GOOD-BYE, ATLANTIS

Marianne Ross

GOOD-BYE, ATLANTIS

ELSEVIER/NELSON BOOKS
New York

No character in this book is intended to
represent any actual person; all the incidents
of the story are entirely fictional in nature.

Library of Congress Cataloging in Publication Data

Ross, Marianne.   Good-bye, Atlantis.

I. Title.
PZ4.R82383Go   [PS3568.O8346]
813'.5'4   79-24535
ISBN 0-525-66670-2

Published in the United States by
Elsevier/Nelson Books, a division of
Elsevier-Dutton Publishing Company, Inc., New York.
Published simultaneously in Don Mills, Ontario,
by Thomas Nelson and Sons (Canada) Limited.

Book design by Ellen LoGiudice
Printed in the U.S.A. First Edition
10 9 8 7 6 5 4 3 2 1

For Morrie
with thanks

One

There are certain people we meet in life who, by virtue of some character trait or persuasion of personality, hold us, and all who follow seem pale and unimportant by comparison.

Such a person, for me, was Jonathan Williamson. I have the strange, unreasonable conviction that he still, even today, inhabits the corridors of Wilson High School, ghostlike and unerasable; that if I were to stoop there and examine closely the hard brown tile floors of that ancient building I would see faint indentations made by the metal clips on his shoes; that from the walls would emanate the faint, unmistakable odor of tobacco; and that if I turned a corner I'd see Jonathan himself—tall and slender, slouching along with his energetic, familiar gait, hands in his pockets.

It seems to me that Jonathan was always there at Wilson, a

permanent fixture like the trophy case and the rumbling waterpipes and the maples, but of course he wasn't. There had to be a time when he, like the rest of us, entered that intrepid building for the first time, a frightened stranger. He came actually the latter part of our sophomore year, transferring from Portland.

In that sophomore year he already began to show signs of leadership, and by his junior year he was firmly entrenched. In his senior year he was as much a part of Wilson as the varnish on the gym floor. For me, Jonathan Williamson is and always will be, as he was then, the student member of the school board. He is and always will be the leader of Wilson, because he thought of the idea of Atlantis.

Atlantis. Jonathan's Atlantis was a combination of ethics, idealism, and illogic, made up chiefly by him, much in the manner that you knit an afghan.

"Always do your best" was the one cardinal rule. There were others, more subjective, but perhaps more important than any rule was Jonathan's belief and insistence that his Atlantis was an actual place that took up space in time, a place more real and valid than the real world, with governing laws stronger than the Constitution or the Ten Commandments. There were no geographical boundaries to this utopian world because there are no geographical boundaries to the heart or soul.

I always saw Jonathan's Atlantis, however, very geographically. It was shaped like our state of Washington, bounded on one side by my home and running west to include Wilson High, then north to Jonathan's house. After that it was bordered by the Soldug River, where we swam in the summer. The climate of Atlantis was the warm climate of eternal summer, in the eighties and nineties. It was green and almost perfectly level like a valley, except for Martha's Peak, which always, always had snow on it. The conditions there were exactly the same as on the day of the Senior Class picnic. It was surrounded, peculiarly, by sparkling blue water like the real Atlantis.

If I were asked to do so today, I could accurately and unhesitatingly draw a real map of Atlantis. It lives in my mind as concretely as the salt maps one makes in childhood of Africa and the United States of America.

For Jonathan, everyone in Wilson High belonged to Atlantis, but I could never believe it. For me, Jonathan's Atlantis was peculiarly his and mine: an island shaped like Washington that we inhabited the year I was eighteen, an island that sank into the sea one day like the real Atlantis as a result of a giant earthquake.

Jonathan was always there, like the dripping maples, and yet I never really saw him until the day before school started in my senior year.

On that day I lay on the bank of the Soldug River, exhausted by the summer and revolted by days of seeking nothing but pleasure. Yet I was too weak of will to resist one last day of sun. It was late afternoon, the kind of day when the sun seems to burn down with peculiar intensity one last time before fall begins. The air was still and sickish with heat; I felt half-dead, sapped of energy. My skin was leathery and dry like a lizard that has lived too long in the sun.

A boy sprinkled sand on my back and I protested feebly, "Go away," feeling my throat fill with disgust.

I had wasted the summer. Wasted three years. My parents

had spoiled me rotten, I thought. They had hopelessly indulged me. They had failed also to teach me the discipline that would have allowed me to achieve anything. Tomorrow school was starting, my senior year, and I had accomplished nothing. Lying in the sun, I felt acutely my deficiencies and the pain of remorse—of opportunities lost, victories never achieved.

It wasn't entirely my parents' fault. In contrast to Jonathan, who was serious, I was by nature happy and frivolous. Going to parties, lying on a sandy beach in the sun, watching men and women fall in love on a movie screen—What was life for if not pleasure?

Another trickle of sand spattered on my shoulder blades. "Go away!" I yelled, and jerked upright. "Oh, hello, Jonathan," I said dully. "I thought it was someone else."

"Such an enthusiastic welcome," Jonathan said, his voice mildly sarcastic. His hair was brushed and neat, cut in exactly the way he liked, so that he looked a little like Prince Valiant. Even on this hot day, he managed to look vibrantly energetic and alive.

"I thought you were in Florida," I said limply. "I thought you weren't coming back."

"Oh. The postcard." He shrugged. "Mother changed her mind."

The postcard had come in July. (*Dear Ann. Having a great time. Mother wants to stay in Florida. May not come back next fall.*) It was the kind of hastily scribbled card you send to many people, because you have promised.

"Glad to see you back." I flopped over onto my stomach. I didn't have the energy to face his enthusiasm, his eagerness for a new year.

10

Jonathan's brown eyes calmly appraised my suntan, which had reached the stage of burned toast. "You look like you've been lying here since the day school let out."

"I have."

His toe banked sand against my arm, then over it, encasing my arm in a plaster cast of gray. Still I didn't move. He continued to look down at me curiously. "Are you coming to school tomorrow, or are you just going to lie here?"

"I may just stay here and die," I mumbled.

"I thought you had a crush on me. I thought you were fascinated by me."

"Likely."

"Don't you even want to hear how I've spent my summer?"

"I'm through with boys. They no longer interest me."

"Are you sick?"

"Just sick of boys."

Jonathan nodded. He picked up a handful of sand and funneled it in a slender gray waterfall through his fingers. "I wish I knew how to cheer you up," he said, sounding genuinely sincere.

"It's all right. Just go away and let me die alone."

"Come back to town. I'll buy you a sundae."

"I'm not hungry." Then I added, "Anyway, I wouldn't be good company. I haven't looked at a book all summer." My brains had probably fried in the summer sun, I thought, atrophied from disuse. I felt my lip tremble with self-pity.

"Let's aim for all A's this year," Jonathan said enthusiastically.

"Are you crazy?" I said in an outraged voice. "I never got better than a B in my life."

"Because you never study," Jonathan said calmly.

"I study. I break my neck studying." It was a lie. I never bothered to take a book home. My grades wavered happily from *B*'s to *D*'s, all perfectly acceptable. "Go away."

He ignored me. Brushing some leaves off the sand, he folded his legs in Indian fashion and sat down beside me.

"In Atlantis people always do their best," he said, looking at me critically.

"Never heard of it."

"You've never heard of Atlantis?"

"No." I sat up in the sand and looked at him, giving him my full attention now. "When did you get back?"

"Yesterday."

"Are you going out for basketball?"

"Probably." Jonathan shrugged. "I haven't decided yet."

It was a typical casual Jonathan remark. He had made the team without effort. Taller than average, a little on the thin side, he possessed a beautiful, long, one-handed shot that started almost midcourt, arched, and then cleared the basket without touching the backboard. Yet he seemed scarcely to care about sports and played almost indifferently, as if it were an afterthought.

"I wouldn't mind playing if I could be good," Jonathan said.

"You're good."

"I mean really good."

"You don't want to be good," I said. "You want to be perfect."

He didn't answer and I repeated flatly, "Not good, *perfect*."

"In Atlantis," Jonathan said simply, "everyone tries to be perfect."

"Never heard of the place," I repeated, putting on my derisive tone to cover up my ignorance.

"You really never heard of Atlantis, Ann?" His voice was filled with disbelief.

I felt myself flush. "No. And neither have you," I mumbled.

"Look it up in the encyclopedia," he challenged.

"There isn't any such place."

"It's a real island that sank into the ocean. The people who lived there had the ideal of perfection."

"So who wants to be perfect?"

Having won, Jonathan grinned a superior boy's grin, uncoiled himself from the sand, and took off in a flying leap. His lithe, athletic body hurtled into the air, arched, and then, in a perfectly fluid motion, his heels dug a mark in the sand.

"You'll beat Akin with a jump like that."

"You miss the whole point, Ann," Jonathan said crisply. "In Atlantis you don't compete to beat someone else. You compete to beat your own mark." He thoughtfully scuffed the toe of his shoe through the sand, his eyebrows furrowed a little, as if his mind were formulating a philosophy. "You aren't good because other people say you should be but only for yourself."

I could feel the idea of Atlantis growing in his mind as we bicycled up the river road and down the darkening streets toward home. Dusk had fallen and the lights of the town were visible in the distance. Overhead, maple leaves made a leafy canopy through which you could look up and see the gray filter of ending daylight. It was the time between day and night when there is a void that seems to belong to no time, and which possesses almost an unreal quality.

13

Through it, Jonathan's mind wound, filling the dusk with an idea of a lost place called Atlantis. His voice was low and serious and had a strangely hypnotizing quality, and as we bicycled through the twilight the landscape underwent a strange metamorphosis. In the subtle way that fantasy becomes reality, it became a no-man's land, neither real nor unreal. Atlantis.

The spell was broken only when we reached the door of my home.

"You all right now?" Jonathan said, looking at my face critically.

I shrugged indifferently. "I'll live."

"I was worried about you for a minute. You looked almost dead."

A small pain formed in my throat. I looked away from his face. "Well, school starts tomorrow," I said lamely.

"Wonder who Penny'll choose for editor of the paper."

His voice betrayed him. He wanted the job. If he didn't get it, I probably would. By rights, I thought, I should get it, but then being a boy gave him a certain edge.

I smiled and said wickedly, "In Atlantis, one does not covet an office. It goes to the most deserving."

"You're right," Jonathan said crisply. "Perfectly right. In Atlantis, filling an office is simply a matter of service." And he turned and walked down the street.

I walked through the house and went directly to the encyclopedia. Atlantis was there: "A large island in the Western Ocean engulfed by the ocean as a result of an earthquake. A utopian commonwealth described by Plato in *Critias*."

14

Two

I have always felt that the Gregorian calendar is wrong. The first day of the year should fall, not on January first, but in September, the day after Labor Day, the first day of school. It is the natural time of beginning. The long warm summer has worn itself out and come to a stale stop; games are old and unexciting; even the air itself seems flat and tired. With fall there comes a quickening in the air, a sharpness; then school begins; everything that is important starts all over.

Filing into assembly in the old Wilson auditorium the following afternoon, I felt my throat fill with the kind of reverence you feel in church. The smells and sounds were so familiar and deafening that they almost overpowered me. No matter how clean it was, the Wilson auditorium always

15

smelled faintly of dust. It wasn't an unpleasant smell—it was like all familiar smells, rather pleasant, evoking old, half-forgotten memories. Everyone in the room was talking, so that a high humming sound rose in the room like a swarm of bees.

The heavy, black velvet curtain slid open on the stage, and Jack Coster walked up the steps. It even seemed right that he was the student-body president, though until that moment I had never really liked him. Behind him came Melvin Akins, the senior-class president, a wiry, conscientious boy whose father managed the Safeway store. I clapped loudly for Akins and less loudly for the junior class officers who, after all, weren't so important.

The auditorium door opened and Jonathan breathlessly came in, late. The familiar clicking of the metal taps on his shoes came down the aisle, and I felt my throat fill again with that particular surprised feeling yesterday had brought, the faint interest in living again.

I couldn't figure out what he was doing on the platform. His glance moved out over the crowd—those brown, scrutinizing eyes—and I felt the shock of recognition and pain deep in my throat as I remembered the long, wasted summer.

Wilson's principal, Mr. Fudnick—we called him Fuddy—wore a gray suit this day. The rest of the year he would wear baggy slacks and sweaters. He had been at Wilson so long that he dispensed with most formalities. There was a spattering of applause as he introduced each class officer, then Jonathan.

"The faculty has chosen Jonathan to be the student-body representative on the school board, a new position this year.

16

He will have no vote, but in every other way he will be an official member. Jonathan Williamson."

"Thank you," Jonathan said. "I appreciate the honor." He nodded his head. "Thank you very much."

His voice was deeper than I thought, older, but then, I remembered, he was a year older than most boys of the senior class. There was some mystery connected to this. Like all newcomers to the school, people had speculated on Jonathan's background. It was rumored that his mother was divorced and very wealthy, that once his father had shut him in a closet for two days, that he had had a nervous breakdown (that was the reason he was a year older than the rest of us).

I looked at him critically as you look at people who mean something to you but not too much. By our standards he was unfashionable. No other boy at Wilson would have been caught dead in a starched white shirt and slacks, or dreamed of wearing metal clips on his shoes. Yet somehow Jonathan got away with it.

In a school dedicated to conformity, he was unique. Although he was on the basketball team, he was more intellectual than athletic. He was active in politics without holding a school office and was a leader at social functions although he seldom had a date.

Fathers liked him for his maturity. For the same reason, mothers found him dangerous. In the arena of the commonplace, which is the small-town public high school, he was that enigma, the boy who belongs to nothing and leads all. All agreed he had a bright future—if he didn't kill himself first, have a mental breakdown, succumb to alcoholism, or die in some tragic way.

I suddenly felt depressed. Yesterday, in the sickening heat,

17

Jonathan's difference had seemed refreshing, appealing. Today he looked like what he'd always been: the oddball, the loner, the underdog champion of lost causes. I didn't want anything to do with oddballs, loners, or underdogs. I wasn't up to it. I wasn't a snob; I just wasn't up to it—the pretense, the strain of being different. The summer had drained me. I couldn't stand to start out the school year with such expenditure of effort.

I looked away, ashamed and a little guilty. It was as if I had been spying on my best friend and had discovered, under carefully applied makeup, a heretofore concealed bad case of acne.

My reverie was stopped by the ending of the assembly and by Fuddy's warning that tomorrow school really started in earnest. Jonathan pushed through the crowd toward me. My depression deepened as I looked into his smiling, happy face. I looked around for help, but everyone else had gone in the opposite direction; the crowd had parted like the Red Sea, leaving Jonathan and me stranded alone.

"Congratulations," I said.

"Congratulations yourself."

I made a noncommittal noise in my throat, feeling awkward.

"You'll make a good editor. Probably better than I would," Jonathan said generously. He said it easily and matter-of-factly, without any trace of envy or memory of last night's conversation. With the remark, all awkwardness ended.

"Thanks."

"You're feeling better today," he said, looking at my face.

"I feel great. I always feel great," I said flippantly.

"All A's this year. Okay?"

"What else?"

He grinned, and I felt myself grinning idiotically back. Our relationship was that of old dear friends who haven't seen each other for a long time. I completely forgot that only a moment before I hadn't really counted him on my list of friends at all.

Akins came through the crowd. "Oh, Jonathan! Got a minute?"

"Sure," Jonathan said. Over his shoulder to me his mouth formed the words, "I'll come over tonight. We'll study. Seven. Okay?"

I stared at him and didn't answer; then he was gone, the clean white of his shirt disappearing in a ring of boys. I went down to the journalism room for some copies of last year's papers and went home.

No one was inside the house, so I went through the sliding glass door to the patio. My mother was sitting in a chair drinking something cool, enjoying the afternoon sun, which poured down on the cement. Both she and my father were good-looking people. In the summer they always had magnificent tans, which made them look healthy and young; I imagined them sometimes as movie stars.

Mother looked up now and smiled. "How was school?"

"I'm the new editor of the paper." I said.

"That's wonderful. Sit down and have a drink, dear." Her voice slid over the two sentences, giving each exactly the same weight.

It meant nothing to her, I realized. A new dress, having a date with a boy, going to a dance—those were the things she understood. But then those were the things I had always desired, too.

"I have to study."

"Oh, surely not today," she protested. "You look so warm. You'll have all year to study."

"No, I have to. I'm aiming for all A's. I intend to be very intellectual and worthy this year."

She laughed, a small, bubbling, amused sound that rose from her throat into the air.

"What's so funny about that?" I said belligerently.

"Nothing. I just can't quite see my darling, beautiful daughter as an intellectual. That's all."

I saw myself through her eyes suddenly, and ambition collapsed. I couldn't see myself in the role either. I looked wistfully at the empty chair with the sunlight flooding down on it. How nice it would be just to relax there with a cool drink until dinner.

I forced myself away and walked upstairs, already feeling the pangs of deprivation, the weight of unwanted resolutions. In a hall mirror, my slender shoulders seemed to sag wearily, too slight to hold up heavy responsibility and high endeavor. Why had I allowed Jonathan to push me into this?

Still, I went up the stairs and almost energetically began to study, buoyed by the thought that Jonathan was coming over tonight. I would show him how I had changed, that I was in earnest. Later in the evening we would turn a record on, dance—

My mind jolted to a stop. Jonathan was not that kind of a boy. Anyway, his interest in me at the moment was purely clinical, a doctor-patient relationship. He had seen me at a moment when I was half-dead in the sun—not as someone to love, but as someone you coaxed back to life, fed tenderly with a spoon.

I had stopped studying entirely and was thinking about Jonathan. It was a novelty, having a boy think of me impersonally, tenderly. It suited my mood. I was sick of the summer, sick of myself. I would show everyone, dazzle them with my brilliance. A beam of light came through the window. Dust motes danced in a stream of white. I stared at them. Be cool and intellectual and high-brow, I decided. Just a little aloof.

Mother called me to dinner. With a start, I realized that I had spent an hour fantasizing and hadn't accomplished anything.

At seven Jonathan came. Coming up the street he walked rather fast, his coat collar flipped up in back, his hair flying in the wind. His body was bent forward a little. I had the strange sensation, watching him, that already the momentum of school had caught him up and was carrying him along like a giant wind.

We worked on the paper—shuffling the dummy sheets around on the coffee table and reshuffling them. The whole thing looked like a puzzle with too many pieces.

"There are too many headlines," Jonathan said, scowling, running his fingers through his hair, rejecting the third dummy sheet. "It looks like a mess."

"I don't see how we're going to get around them."

Last year's editors hadn't solved the problem either. The first edition had started out triumphantly with a bold black headline across the top announcing the beginning of school. Then it faltered downward to another black head and finally gave up entirely, with pictures of class officers and headlines scattered indiscriminately anywhere they fell, as if the editor had suddenly been defeated by the enormity of the project.

Suddenly Jonathan had an inspiration. He took away the large headlines and balanced the page with two medium-size headlines. He grouped the class officers on one side of the page and put the single picture of himself on the other. With staggered heads, the effect was one of perfect balance and proportion, neat and geometric. It also gave his picture the lead spot. I noticed that, too.

But the total effect was right. And Jonathan was too modest ever to be accused of trying to capture the headlines, I thought. We were in the midst of congratulating ourselves on our brilliance when the phone rang.

"Ann—it's for you," Mother called, and I walked into the living room to answer it.

Carol Marshall, my best friend, was on the other end of the line. "Something terrible has happened!" she screamed.

My heart gave one hard alarmed jolt against my chest. I thought of a car wreck. I thought that something had happened to her parents. The two thoughts came in that order.

"Fuddy's dead," Carol sobbed.

"Fuddy?" I echoed, shocked as if Wilson had burned down in the night.

"He was going down to the basement to work on the furnace, and he had a heart attack. There must have been too much excitement and pressure . . . the beginning of school . . ." Her voice trailed away.

I couldn't believe it. Fuddy.

"They're going to have services for him in the school auditorium," Carol said, still sobbing.

I went back into the rec room.

"Fuddy's dead," I said.

"Fuddy?" Jonathan echoed.

22

Looking at his face, I felt shock almost as great as the shock of Fuddy's death. His face, only a moment before triumphant and exuberant with heightened color, looked stricken. The color had drained entirely out of it, leaving a washed-out gray, as if he had been ill for a long time, a convalescent who never saw the sun. The growth of a day's beard heightened this effect.

"What's going to happen, Ann?" His slender hands, always animated and in motion, lay perfectly still in his lap. He looked stunned and bewildered. It was the first time I had seen him lose composure. Then I realized the reason for it. Fuddy and he had had a close relationship, more like father and son than principal and student. He had definitely been Fuddy's favorite.

I began to cry softly, filled with soft regret for the old man who had ruled the halls of Wilson in his old faded sweaters and baggy pants.

Jonathan, startled, looked at me silently. The color came back into his face, although it remained sober.

"Fuddy had a long life," he said quietly. "I think he had a good life." I nodded and felt the wave of grief pass. In that moment Jonathan, only a year older, was a mature adult, I a child. Jonathan continued to look down at his hands. "Maybe it's better to die this way. My father had a stroke. In the end he was nothing."

It was something he hadn't meant to say. The words hung in the room between us, and I had the feeling he wanted to snatch them back. His hands actually gave a jerk upward as if he might physically pluck the words from the air and put them back in his mouth. Then his hands fell back again, and he remained rigid, staring at them.

I was stunned. I didn't know what to say. I had always

believed the school gossip that Jonathan's mother and father were divorced, that his father had locked him in the closet for two days when he was a child. Those things weren't true at all. His father had died of a stroke and had ended up as nothing.

I rose stiffly and did the first thing that came to my mind, I took the popcorn bowl out into the kitchen and refilled it. When I came back Jonathan was composed again. We silently finished laying out the paper on the dummy sheet and then, still sobered by the fact of death, said good night.

He closed the door softly behind him and walked down the street. I watched him disappear from sight at the end of the block, and the first day of school ended.

At Fuddy's funeral Friday I cried again. He was the first important person in my life who had ever died. I sat with a group of other girls and felt the wetness roll down my cheeks—the soft, almost pleasurable tears of a girl—because, of course, I knew nothing of death, nothing of real sorrow or grief.

Fuddy's death was practically the only subject people talked about the next few days at Wilson. Students huddled in the hallways in groups and remembered him. It set a solemn tone to a year that otherwise might have been ordinary. We were prepared to sacrifice, to be better than we were, for the kindly old man who had ruled Wilson. Then gradually the natural order of things took over again. Sorrow turned to speculation as to what would happen now.

At this late stage of the year, who would replace Fuddy? Raymond Summers suggested gleefully one day that perhaps they wouldn't be able to get a replacement. Nobody ever listened to Raymond Summers. He was an art student, intelligent, but a rather effeminate boy who looked and acted as if he were gay—although at that age I wasn't exactly sure what being gay meant.

The thought of being without a principal took dizzying root for a few days, due to our natural desire for disorder. We speculated on the delightful possibility of a school without authority, then plummeted back to reality when the Superintendent of Schools announced that starting on Monday Gary Herrider was going to be the new principal of Wilson.

Gary Herrider. What kind of a name was that for a principal? But of course we had been used to Fuddy. We were prepared to hate any replacement.

Herrider's primary targets were old teachers, the Journalism Department, and Jonathan. Almost the first day he singled Jonathan out as the enemy. Perhaps it was the white starched shirt or the taps on his shoes or his easy, older assurance. Perhaps Herrider saw in all that some insolence, some threat to him.

He came out of his office and cornered Jonathan in the hall.

"What's your name?"

Jonathan and I were out of class, going downtown to see about getting some ads for the paper.

"Your name?" he repeated sharply.

Jonathan seemed too surprised to answer, then did. "Jonathan Williamson."

"I really don't think taps on shoes are necessary," Herrider said coolly.

Jonathan didn't answer.

"Please get rid of them by tomorrow."

"Yes, sir," Jonathan said. A red line of color rose above his collar line. He started to move on, and Herrider stopped him.

"Just a minute, Williamson."

The color in Jonathan's face deepened.

"You're the student representative on the school board?"

"Yes, sir."

"This was a faculty selection?"

"Yes, sir—that is, I believe so—maybe Fuddy had something to do with it—"

"Fuddy—you mean Mr. Fudnick."

"Yes."

Herrider smiled indulgently. "I plan to have a more democratic school than Mr. Fudnick. We'll put it up to a student-body vote, I think."

"Yes, sir. Is there anything else?"

The principal looked at him.

"No, I think that's all, Williamson. The taps, remember?"

"Taps. Right."

Jonathan clicked his heels together. They made a sharp *clip* sound like a Gestapo salute.

Herrider opened his mouth, then shut it again. He looked at me.

"And where are you going?"

"Downtown—to get some ads," I stammered, "for the paper. Penny—"

"*Miss* Penny gave you permission?"

"Yes, we always—"

"I'll have to talk to some of these older teachers about some of these things. Well, all right. After this, ask for permission from me."

Clippety-clip—Jonathan's heels went down the hallway.

26

In the place where humiliation is born, I felt the stir of anger. "The new regime," I muttered. "Good-bye, Atlantis."

"Not necessarily," Jonathan said stiffly. He was walking very straight. It gave him an unbalanced, wooden look, as if he were walking on stilts. We walked another block in silence, the unnatural flushed color gradually leaving Jonathan's face.

"He doesn't like me," he said.

I looked at him sharply. I had never thought it was necessary for Jonathan to be liked. He always seemed composed, indifferent to criticism.

"He doesn't even know you."

"He doesn't like Penny either. Or Casey."

"How do you know that?"

"Casey and Penny were talking about it in their room when I came in this morning. Herrider doesn't like old teachers. He's going to make it miserable for them in the hope that they'll quit."

"Penny and Casey? They're practically institutions," I protested.

"I think we should draw up an Atlantis Charter," Jonathan said stiffly.

I looked at him and didn't answer. Atlantis Charter. It had seemed to me that Atlantis was just an idea that had included the two of us, but it seemed awkward saying that out loud, and selfish, so I didn't say anything.

Jonathan was frowning, his thinking kind of frown. "I'll round up the class officers and as many others as I can and we'll meet tonight at Pete's."

That night the Atlantis Charter was born—out of death, humiliation, and Jonathan's anger.

"Every class, it seems to me, has a certain character,"

Jonathan said, looking around the crowded table at the pizza parlor. "Last year's class was known for its wildness. Everyone knows that. The class before that was conservative. Our class needs to stand for something, too."

"You're right," Coster, the student-body president, agreed. "We should stand for something special."

"I propose that we draw up a charter," Jonathan said. "The Atlantis Charter." He looked around the table. "Atlantis, for those of you who don't know, was a utopian commonwealth that Plato wrote about. It was an island that sank into the sea as a result of an earthquake. We'll make our class the idealistic class, the class that stands on principle. Everyone in it works toward the Greek ideal of perfection."

"What do we do," Arthur Langley said gloomily, "besides stand around and try to be perfect?"

Everyone laughed.

"We take a positive stand on issues," Jonathan said. "That's the point. We don't just stand around being a do-nothing class. We take positive action. We live up to the ideals of Atlantis."

"Sounds okay. Sounds good," Akins said.

"Everybody here tonight will be a charter member of Atlantis," Jonathan said.

"What about the rest of the class?" Coster asked.

"Atlantis is an idea, not a formal group. We'd like, of course, the whole class to live by the idea. Principally, it's up to the individual." He looked at me.

"I think the first issue we take up should be Casey and Penny," I said. "We're not going to let them be run out of Wilson."

"That's right," Jonathan said. "We'll put on positive

pressure. As a member of the school board, I'll take it there if necessary."

Everyone agreed in principle.

"If this is going to be the Atlantis Charter, shouldn't we have a charter scroll?" Akins suggested.

"Exactly right," Jonathan said crisply. "We want it to be official." I don't think the thought had occurred to him until that moment. He produced a piece of paper and began to write on it. "The essential ingredient, I believe, is that an individual does his best," he said. "He always aims for the highest—in sports, scholastically, and ethically. I'll write that on top." He listed five or six other rules others suggested and ended with the words, "All members promise to abide by the rules and principles of Atlantis outlined in the charter meeting."

"We'll all sign it," he said solemnly, signing his own name on the top.

"I'll take it home and make it a real scroll," Raymond Summers offered. "There should be a cord to hang it by."

"Good!" said Jonathan.

Everyone ordered hamburgers. Jonathan stood talking to Raymond Summers. Looking at Jonathan's back, Coster said to Akins, "Well, what do you think of the idea of Atlantis?"

"I wouldn't tell Williamson, but I think the whole thing is a bunch of hogwash," Akins said, grinning.

"Pure unadulterated crap," Coster said.

"What'd you sign it for?"

"I don't know. Why'd you?"

They looked at each other, smiled, and shrugged.

"You know Jonathan," Akins said.

I stared at them. They saw me and moved away.

The meeting broke up, and everyone was pleased. It was the kind of satisfaction that comes with making New Year's Eve resolutions, exchanging blood oaths, and wearing secret rings. Since we didn't know yet the pain of standing by an ideal, it was rather like a social meeting. And of course at that age, we knew little of consequences.

It was a night for important decisions, shoe-black, with clouds hanging somberly in the sky. Jonathan, walking me home after the meeting, said, "I think it went pretty well, don't you?" We were walking along a street lined with trees; the lights of old stately houses shone back at us, the dull, familiar lights of the town where I had been born. "Yes, I think it went pretty well," I said in a low voice.

One of the differences between the two of us, which I was to notice many times, was that I went along with things to please others; Jonathan believed in them. He carried others along by the sheer weight of his own belief.

In reality, Jonathan was a dinosaur who belonged to another age. I have often visualized him in a toga with sandals, a Greek citizen stopping in the town square to discuss philosophy and morals with other men. He would have fitted in perfectly with that time.

Yet, in some strange way, the idea of Atlantis did fit, and even Jonathan himself did. Nobody would have wanted to emulate him; nevertheless, he stood for that part of each of us that wanted to be best, that secret part that wanted to be noble, above pettiness, ideal in some way that men have never learned to be. That was the reason Atlantis could become a reality.

Under Jonathan's guidance, our senior class became as distinctive as the two classes above it. We were not the wild

30

ones, the class whose red paint still stood vulgarly on highway posts and water towers and train underpasses, and we were not the pale conservatives of two years past whose faces were already hard to remember. We were Greeks who discussed and decided issues on the basis of morality. The year itself has a yellow haze around it; it was a golden year that stands apart from all other years.

Three

T he following weeks I was happy, and I threw myself into study with all the dedication of one who has sinned heavily, repented, and given himself over to religious good works.

Since discipline wasn't natural to me, I had to work late every night, and even then barely kept up. Every night, without fail, there was German vocabulary to learn and two pages of math problems to do. For English there was a weekly book report and composition. I was assured of an A from Penny in journalism because I was editor, but all my other subjects were in jeopardy.

I lost weight, looked wild-eyed, and went around the house muttering German conjugation. *Ich bin, du bist, er ist.*

My parents were alarmed.

"We're proud of your—ah—efforts, but don't you think

you are overdoing it?" my father said one evening at dinner.

"I intend to get all A's this year," I announced, and triumphantly stabbed at a carrot.

My father threw back his head and laughed. He had a very pleasant laugh, and he looked handsome under the soft table light. At forty, he was still attractive and a little vain about it.

"Very laudable," he said, sobering abruptly, clearing his throat.

"Oh, really, Andy, look at her!" Mother said despairingly. "She's beginning to look like a pale little ghost!"

This was hardly true, since my tan had barely faded, but my eyes were hollow and circled from lack of sleep.

"Such is the price of fame," I said loftily. I felt especially elated this evening. I had gotten an A in my German test.

"Make her get some exercise," Mother begged. "Tell her she must eat."

"Is it that boy?" my father said gently, peering at me.

"Of course not," I said impatiently. "I'm just tired of this life we lead. I'm tired of being *nothing*." My voice trembled with feeling as I thought of the years wasted, the hours spent on nothing but pleasure.

Pleasure was a way of life for my parents. My father worked, of course, but evenings and weekends were devoted to planning the next moment of pleasure—a new place to eat, a weekend holiday, a party, the friends they would invite who would be compatible and fun. What was life for if not pleasure? Up to now that had been my own motto, too.

"You don't understand," I said, my voice trembling a little. "I have to work hard or I'll never make it. I have to work harder than the others because I have such a history of—moronity!"

I blurted it out accusingly, bitterly. And it was true. I had found almost immediately that nobody took my intellect seriously. Teachers like Casey looked at my marks skeptically and assumed that I had cheated, or that it was a fluke.

"Moronity," my father repeated, staring at me. Like most vain people he never doubted his intelligence or his superior qualities in all areas.

"Yes. Moronity," I said in a flat voice.

"I agree with your mother. You're taking all this much too seriously," my father said. "A senior year is meant to be fun, honey—boys, dances, parties. There's time enough when you grow up to be serious."

I flung my napkin on the table and leaped to my feet. I was too agitated to think.

"You've spoiled me rotten. I hate you for it!" I said in a trembling voice.

And I rushed upstairs. No doubt I was nervous and unstrung from worry and an overworked brain. Even as I flung myself on the bed I realized that it was more myself I hated than them. Through the walls I heard the sound of their voices, and then finally the TV went on as they ceased to worry about me and gave themselves over to the pleasure of being amused.

The familiar sounds of the house lulled me like a ballad of lost love. I opened a book, my fingers trembling a little, and stared at the words: "The desire to mean something in the world is stronger than food, money, or even life." I couldn't make the words mean anything to me; I heard in my mind the plaintive echo of summer. The memory of sun-filled days flooded my senses: birds shrieking at a morning window, the rough texture of sand against my cheek, a sunburned body dropping silently into cool water.

34

My mind formed words I would say to Jonathan tomorrow. "Look, Jonathan, it's a great idea, but I'm not really cut out for all A's. Look, Jonathan, it was fun while it lasted, but now—ha-ha—" <del>C880017</del>O. SCHOOLS

I swung my mind severely back to the book, gave up, and tried German conjugation.

"Great. Simply great!"—Jonathan's words. Jonathan who believed in Atlantis, Jonathan who believed in being one's best. He had stood on the steps of Wilson on Wednesday, peering at the A on my paper. A flick of pride, bright and shining as a steel sword, had pierced my soul with his words.

But in the end my natural desire for pleasure won. I suppose it could have been predicted. One does not change overnight. I had gone up to my room to study but found excuses to postpone the drudgery. Cluttered room, cluttered mind, I thought, and I pared down the room to monk severity—bare bed, neat bookshelves, a desk that held only a lamp and a row of books. All of this to postpone an English composition. The room, after its transformation, looked somewhat like a prison. But then, for me, it was a prison.

"Once upon a time I was happy," I doodled tentatively on the top of a blank piece of paper, and then stared at the words, shocked, because they expressed my true feelings.

Because once I had been happy, I thought. Once I had been free and happy—and natural. It was unnatural to force the brain to such effort; it wasn't normal to sit in a stuffy little room every night conjugating German. Cliques were as normal as natural selection; it was unnatural to smile and be nice to everyone.

"*Humanum est errare*," I said aloud. To err is human. It was a new Latin phrase that I planned to try out on Jonathan.

"Once upon a time I was happy." I wrote it again, boldly, and then the words poured out of me. They came easily, because I knew so well what had once made me happy: the soft pleasures that came from lack of restraint or discipline, the feel of summer, the feel of cool wind in a car with the top down, the touch of a boy's hand.

In the composition I wrote, summer ended, school started, and a girl was sent away to a strict school. Forced to study, she could only look out her window back to the time of happiness. It was my life, of course, fictionalized only in minor ways. Penny gave me an A on the paper. Jonathan read it and handed it back silently, unimpressed. I suppose he felt it was some sort of personal criticism.

"I thought you wanted to change," he said, looking at me with a faintly perplexed half-frown on his face. "I thought you wanted to be a student this year."

"I got an A, didn't I?"

"That isn't the point."

"What is the point?"

"The point is the paper expresses a completely warped sense of values. I don't see how anyone can live that way, can actually believe that is happiness."

"It's just a paper," I said sullenly. "It doesn't mean that I want to live that way."

"You're right," Jonathan said, relenting a little. "I'm probably just jealous."

"Probably," I said stiffly.

"I have to go down and practice basketball. Want to wait for me?"

"I better get home and study German," I said a little bitterly.

His reaction had left me depressed. I had thought he would be pleased, proud of me. It was disconcerting, too, to have him lash out at what to me had been a perfectly satisfactory way of life for eighteen years. And I had been happy, I thought with a pang of longing. Maybe it was superficial and frivolous, but I had been happy.

I went home, but I didn't study. There was no need to overdo it. I had all week before the next German test.

My father came up to my room, smiling, in good spirits. "I've brought you a present," he said. "Catch!" He tossed a package in my direction.

I caught it and immediately felt in a better mood. I loved getting presents, and my parents were fond of buying them for me. A pair of earrings, a stuffed animal, a little bottle of wine—such things were their way of saying they loved me when they went away alone for a holiday.

"A jogging suit," I said, pleased, holding up a white pair of pants and handsome jacket.

"Now you can go out in the morning and get a little exercise," my father said. "In style." He smiled. "All work, no play makes Ann a dull girl, you know."

"It's beautiful," I said, touching the material. It was expensive and lovely.

He left, and I pulled on the pants and jacket. By nature vain, I noted with pleasure that the clothes fit perfectly and were flattering. I went downstairs, admired myself in the hall mirror, and then jogged down the block. No one was in sight, but it was pleasant running in the cool air. I decided that I would get up early tomorrow and jog. All work, no play makes Ann a dull girl, as my father said. "Clean mind, clean body," I added.

The following morning I got up at six. I jogged past Jonathan's house, hoping he would be up. He wasn't, so I went down to the park, then looped back, jogging very slowly past the big old white house where he lived. It was a castlelike structure with turrets and pillars and wide porches, and it was known in town as the Merritt house.

"Hey, great!" a voice called out a window, and a moment later Jonathan came clattering down the front steps, dragging on a jacket as he ran.

He loped along beside me, throwing exclamations into the air as he ran. "Really great—get in shape—ought to do this every morning!" His words were like small smoke signals rising intermittently into the frosty air.

We came to a shuddering stop finally, gasping for breath.

"How long you been doing this?" Jonathan said.

"Just this morning. I plan to jog every morning," I said, only now making the decision.

"Mind if I jog with you?"

I hesitated. "No, I guess not."

"Good. Meet me at my house tomorrow at six thirty."

"Sure. Okay. Glad to have company," I mumbled.

He raised his hand in a little wave and jogged off, his hair sticking up in strange little tufts on his head. I stared after him for a moment and then headed for home.

So, clumsily, almost unobtrusively, he worked his way into my life that winter, like a mild conqueror taking possession of one territory after another, until he finally possessed it all. Perhaps he instinctively understood what I knew only later, that it was what I had wanted all the time. One can only be conquered if one surrenders, and long before he conquered, I had voluntarily surrendered.

My impression of Jonathan changed over the weeks—not changed so much actually as widened. My initial, superficial impression of him as an oddball deepened to a feeling that naturally he was an oddball; all people of worth were oddballs. *Normal*, by its very definition, meant sameness, lack of difference, and a certain lack of originality. Jonathan was unique. Even to the most casual observer, he stood out as someone totally different.

This I had always attributed to physical differences. He had distinct mannerisms; for example, the way he held a pencil. He didn't let it sag into the hollow between the thumb and forefinger as most people do, but instead held it in an almost perfectly perpendicular position so that his writing had a soldierly straightness about it.

His hands always held a pencil as he talked. The eraser rested on his cheek, was poised in midair, or perched on his ear. The pencil was such an integral part of him that you felt almost that it was an appendage. Life seemed to flow from Jonathan's fingertips down into the pencil where his true being was expressed. Just as some people watch a person's eyes closely, finding them a barometer of his moods, I often found myself staring intently at Jonathan's fingers and the pencil held in them.

As I came to know him better I realized that the difference in Jonathan was not a matter of physical difference so much as one of depth. At some place in their personalities, boys like Coster and Akins seemed to end. Jonathan continued to go on. It was as if his personality were made up of layer after layer, like rock strata, one layer peeling off only to reveal another, deeper, vein.

Jonathan, while belonging to Wilson as much as any boy

could, always seemed to be in touch with some larger world, a world that extended far beyond Rockfort or Washington or the United States. Sometimes I had the impression that Jonathan, at nineteen, had already lived many lives. He understood instinctively things about life that the rest of us had only begun to grasp.

Yet in many ways Jonathan was as provincial as the rain forests in Washington. He adored building things—kites, skateboards, stilts, anything that could be hammered together—and he loved chocolate sundaes. But everything that he did, of course, ended up in one way or another as competition. Instead of jogging we ended up with a few fast dashes and a mile.

"What are we training for, the Olympics?" I said one morning—one of those incredible clean-bright Washington mornings when Mount Rainier rose out of the earth like a giant apparition and the sky was cold and absolutely blue. I wobbled to a stop, breathing heavily.

Jonathan clicked a stopwatch and peered down at it. "Just seeing how fast we're going."

I sank down on a curb. "Fifty-five's the speed limit," I said, making a feeble joke. "Tell me if we go faster than that."

"Tired?"

"Certainly not," I said sarcastically. "My legs are shaking like leaves, my lungs are breaking—but other than that I'm in perfect shape."

"You're getting to be a pretty good runner. You'd do well in track."

"I'm not the athletic type," I said limply.

"You didn't think you were the scholastic type either," Jonathan reminded me.

"Isn't it enough to be brilliant? Must I be Superwoman, too?"

Jonathan grinned. "Wouldn't you like a few trophies lining the walls? Glittering gold. Silver. Track is very in for girls now."

"Doesn't tempt me."

"What about just the honor of the school?" Jonathan said.

"Ugh."

"Good old Wilson . . ."

"What happened to good old fun? Good old jogging for fun?"

"Okay." He raised his hand. "Okay. Forget it. Forget I mentioned it."

"I appreciate your faith in my ability, but—I decline." I stretched my legs out.

"Decline. Absolutely all right in Atlantis to decline. Good old jogging for fun. Won't mention the other again."

But he did, of course. He kept a stopwatch on the girls trying out for track and decided I could go faster, and I found myself doing what he wanted, as I always did, because he always made it seem unreasonable not to. In Atlantis one always did one's best. One always aimed at the high mark. It was Jonathan's cardinal rule.

The added effort brought rewards. Sometimes the clean joy of achieving broke in my chest like a brilliant display of fireworks on the Fourth of July, Roman candles and skyrockets rising up in the sky in a clean, pure, perfect line. On these rare occasions I felt a humble gratitude to Jonathan because I knew that without him I would have wasted the year. I didn't have the will not to.

Other times I felt a childish resentment. Before Jonathan,

I had been perfectly happy and natural; he had perverted my true nature. One night after a race, I flopped on the bed and lay there half-dead from exhaustion, staring at the walls, one hand draped over the side of the bed.

Why should I, who had always been free and happy, force myself to the point of exhaustion to win a trophy, an A? It wasn't normal to do one's best; it was normal to be weak and make mistakes and indulge oneself in the soft pleasures of the senses. To flirt and dance and make love lightly, and know it meant nothing. It wasn't normal to be like Jonathan, I thought.

The thought startled me. Because who was more normal than Jonathan? Jonathan aiming for some invisible high mark—wasn't that what all of us, in our secret hearts, wanted: to be the best?

I roused myself from my lethargy, showered, and went downstairs to eat dinner.

"You look exhausted," my mother said. "Look at her, Andy. She can hardly walk she's so tired."

"I'm all right," I said. "Really. It's just the race."

"Racing, studying all hours of the night—" My father's eyes were concerned. "Where's my little girl who used to go to dances and parties?"

I smiled wanly and didn't answer. The tone of his voice made me want to cry. I looked out the window.

Winter had come to Wilson almost effortlessly, as if summer had made a mistake and forgotten to end. The mornings were crisp now, that was the only difference. The real winter had forgotten to materialize. Creek banks, usually overflowing, gurgled at a sleepy level; people complained that there was no snow pack and reveled in the sunshine, walking around the streets in shirt sleeves and light jackets. The approach of Thanksgiving season caught Wilson, along with everyone else, by surprise.

For the sport figures of Wilson there had been football. For fans like myself Friday nights were reserved always for the game. Saturday night, falling into a lazy routine, Jonathan and I worked on the paper, studied German, and played cribbage at my house.

He never indicated that it was anything more than school business, and I never admitted that it was anything more than that either. In Wilson the word "love" was gauche, and I wouldn't have been caught dead saying it about Jonathan Williamson even if it had applied. In this case it didn't, since we were simply the best of friends. He never parked or tried to make out; we were simply good friends.

Atlantis was now entrenched in Wilson as firmly as if it had always been there. For the first time in school history there was heavy competition for grades as well as sports, and regular Atlantis Charter meetings were held. Jonathan had made the type of school he wanted, the type of school in which he excelled.

Of course. He had originated the idea, hadn't he? I had to admit it showed off his abilities remarkably well. Athletically alone, he wasn't strong enough to shine; both athletically and scholastically, he was the acknowledged leader. We all followed him like sheep.

The first major dance of the year, the senior dance, was the first break in what could have been called Jonathan's absolute reign. Suddenly the soldiers broke ranks, forgot studies, and talked about whom they were going to the dance with, what they were going to wear.

I had decided to be stoic and not mention the dance to Jonathan, but as we sat playing cribbage one evening it was almost the first thing I said.

"You going to the dance Saturday?"

"I don't know," Jonathan said. "Probably not." He paused, looking up from the cribbage board, his slender fingers still resting on one of the pegs. There was no expression on his face to indicate that it made any difference to him whether he went or not. "Why?"

"No reason."

"You going?"

"Probably not." Since I was with Jonathan almost every day, it wasn't likely any other boy would ask me.

There was a little silence, as if it had just occurred to him that I might like to be asked. He lifted the peg and put it into a hole.

"I might help with the decorations."

I stifled a pang of disappointment and put my peg in a hole.

There was a longer silence. We finished the game.

"If you want to go, we'd just as well go," Jonathan said carelessly.

My heart gave a happy leap against my chest, like something let out of prison. "Go to the dance?"

"Wasn't that what we were talking about?"

"Are your asking me?"

"That's what I'm doing, asking you."

"I'm not sure I can go. I halfway promised to baby-sit for the Thompsons."

"Gosh, that's too bad," Jonathan said. He sounded genuinely sorry, and looked at my face closely, searching for disappointment.

"You could have asked me last Saturday," I said stiffly. "You didn't have to wait until the last minute."

Jonathan looked at me queerly. "I didn't know you were counting on it so," he said. "I didn't know these things meant so much to you, Ann."

"They don't mean so much to me," I said in a flat voice. "I wasn't *counting* on it."

"You were, though," Jonathan said. "I can tell by your face."

"I wasn't *counting* on it. I would rather have gone to the dance than spend the night baby-sitting."

"I'm sorry. I really am," Jonathan said, and I saw that it was the truth; he was genuinely sorry. It hadn't even occurred to him that I might want to go.

The thought of going to the dance was too much of a temptation to resist. I had a vision of myself swooping gracefully across the floor in a long dress, while Jonathan fended off my admirers. I would have to skip school, go to Seattle, buy a new formal.

And Casey's test? Without a qualm, I traded a new formal for an A.

"I can probably get out of the baby-sitting," I said.

I am ashamed to say it—it sounds so frivolous now—but I spent all of the next week happily thinking about the dance and didn't study at all. The girls in my group cared nothing for intellectual things. All had the same simple goals: to wear a boy's ring and go to all the school dances. So what could you expect?

Mother loved shopping and met me downtown after school every night and we browsed through the shops looking at formals. Finally on Wednesday we agreed that Thursday afternoon we'd go to Seattle and look in the bigger shops. I'd have to skip school and Casey's test, but I had missed school many times before in previous years.

"I'll come home at noon," I said. "You can write a slip and say I was sick."

"I suppose we'll have to," Mother said. "I hate lying, but—all right, this one time."

She could not resist, either, the thought of a dance or buying a new formal. She had been very popular herself as a girl; on occasions like this we would sit and eat lunch in an expensive place and she would tell me about her own boyfriends. It made us seem more like friends than mother and daughter; she looked gay and young and pretty and I could see why my father had fallen in love with her.

"I think the white one," she said this day. "It sets off your tanned shoulders beautifully."

"I agree. It's so expensive, though. Dad will have a fit."

"Well, it isn't every day you get to go to a dance. Someday this will all be over," she said, sighing.

It made her seem old suddenly. I hated the thought of being old, of never going to parties again. Having the natural egotism of the young, I shrugged off the thought as something that was too far away in the future to worry about and thought happily again about the formal.

All went well until class the next day. Casey, with her naturally suspicious mind, told me that I looked remarkably well—considering that yesterday I had been so ill.

I flushed and shifted my weight from one foot to the other.

"It must have been the twenty-four-hour flu," she said.

"Yes," I said eagerly. "That's what it must have been."

"It comes every year about this time. Just before the dance."

"I was really sick," I said.

"I'm sure you were," she said dryly, "but just so no one will cry favoritism, I suggest you write a five-hundred-word report on the energy crisis, like the others."

"Others?" I stammered.

"The others who had the same—uh, flu."

I hated being caught; I hated the thought of having to write a five-hundred-word report. "I was really sick," I said.

"That'll be all, Ann. Thank you."

Jonathan followed me out of the room. I could see he was angry.

"What did you have to lie for?" he said furiously.

"I was really si——"

"Oh, for crying out loud. Don't lie again. You've been talking all morning about what you did yesterday!" He was walking swiftly ahead of me down the hallway. Angry at me for lying, he burst out impatiently, "What good does it do to have something like the Atlantis Charter if nobody follows it?"

I felt myself flush.

"It isn't enough to have rules. There should be penalties," Jonathan said.

"What do you propose—ten lashes?" I was surprised by the bitterness in my voice. I had skipped school for only four hours, telling only a small white lie about being sick. The fact that I had been caught by Casey was galling; the fact that he was challenging me on top of it was unbearable. I was sick of trying to be perfect.

"Not ten lashes," Jonathan said impatiently. "Of course not. But I think there should be some penalty."

"For me," I said in a flat voice.

"You, and me, too, if I break the rules."

But of course, that was easy for him to say. He was the one who thought of most of the rules. It wasn't likely he'd break his own rules.

"What do you suggest?" I said bleakly.

"How about taking away something we really want?"

He certainly seemed eager enough, I thought, when it was I who was involved. I continued to look at him, thoughts forming vaguely in my mind. I felt guiltily, too, that he was right.

"I suppose I could skip the show tonight," I mumbled.

"You're not that keen on going to a Western anyway, are you?"

"Seems all right to me," I muttered.

"It wouldn't really be a penalty, though, don't you see?"

"All right," I said sullenly, "I won't go to the dance." I looked at him defiantly. There. I hope you're satisifed. I won't go to the dance. I'll punish myself by not going to the dance.

"Good," Jonathan said, "And if I break a rule I'll drop out of basketball for a week."

Nobody could say it wasn't fair. I had to admit that. Still, it was I who had broken the rules of Atlantis, not he. I noted that, too, in my mind, as I stared at him bitterly.

"There's no reason you shouldn't go to the dance because I can't go," I said rather stiffly.

I thought he would say that naturally he wouldn't think of going with anyone else. Instead he said, "I suppose it's too late now," in what I thought was a disappointed tone.

"You could ask Carmen Matia," I said, and laughed hoarsely. Carmen was a cute little Spanish girl who had entered the school a month ago. Her mother was a professional dancer, and Carmen herself had done a dancing number for a school assembly, complete with tambourine, skimpy costume, and clicking castanets.

Jonathan flushed.

"Or Raymond Summers," I shot out, going on recklessly.

"What's that supposed to mean?" Jonathan said coldly.

"Nothing," I said sullenly.

The point I really meant to make was that he spent an awful lot of time with Raymond Summers. There had been the Atlantis scroll, then collaboration on artwork for the paper—I didn't really know what I meant. I remembered the gossip about Raymond's being gay, and suddenly I wanted desperately to get off the subject.

Jonathan continued to look at me. Then his face went blank and adult, and it was impossible to tell what he was thinking. "I probably won't go," he said indifferently. A few minutes later, making some excuse, he left. I watched his retreating slouching figure swing down the hall and felt a pang of regret. I felt as though we'd been quarreling. The autumn had been so perfect, and now we were quarreling.

It was a warning I should have heeded, but I didn't. As if to emphasize the point, a bell now rang deep in the recesses of Wilson, and I stood listening to it for several seconds before I moved.

In class, I barely listened to the teacher's voice. My mind circled like a buzzard over the miserable day, hoping to salvage something from the wreckage. It occurred to me that maybe by now Jonathan had changed his mind, and I wandered down to the gym to find him.

Raymond Summers was the chairman of decorations. He had painted scenes of waterfalls and rocks and built a wishing

49

well in the center of the gym floor, and Jonathan and he were supervising the hanging of crepe-paper streamers and the lighting effects. As I entered the gym that afternoon they were engrossed in the project, kneeling on the floor, their two heads bent over a wall mural.

Something about the way they knelt there held my attention. It was an innocent-enough scene: two boys bent over a large piece of paper. They rose now and Jonathan put his arm on Raymond's shoulder. My heart began to beat with unnatural fastness. The simple gesture seemed somehow obscene; Jonathan, who believed in Atlantis, touching Raymond Summers. How could he bear even to speak to him?

I had intended to go into the gym and see Jonathan. Instead I backed out of the doorway, turned, and walked in the opposite direction, planning some new errand. My heart was beating very fast. When I reached the end of the hall I felt as if I had been running, as if everyone were staring at me, although in reality I had actually turned very calmly and walked down the hall, and nobody was looking at me at all.

Four

I n that year when I loved Jonathan Williamson, there is a strange ambiguity. I both wanted Jonathan to win and to fail.

Although he was more of a student than an athlete, my strongest memories are of him as an athlete: Jonathan arching a basketball into a hoop with one hand; Jonathan rising at the end of a slim pole to a point in space, then flinging himself over a bar.

Always I see him arched in an attitude of grace, slenderly poised on the earth, ready to fling himself at some high point. I never see him failing—although he did many times. It always seems to me that he is that unique individual who is so in tune with his environment that he defies it, defies the natural order of things; never fails, never falls, never makes a clumsy move.

51

Yet strangely, too, another strong memory of that year is the memory of myself waiting for him to fall. Someday Jonathan the Perfect would fall, and then I would let him know that I had known all the time, hadn't been fooled.

I wasn't a natural student. Every time I sat down to a desk to study it was with reluctance. Every hour of discipline was a perversion of my true nature, which was fun-loving, unrestricted, and pleasure-seeking. In the solitude of my room, I resented Jonathan's effortless ease of achievement, his tyranny. With winter my mind became sluggish, my will flagged. Locked in the winter days of cold and ice, I longed to be released into spring. Frustrated, I longed for Jonathan to fall.

Then one day, incredibly, he did. I don't believe it ever occurred to Jonathan that other people might resent his victories or successes. He himself enjoyed competition. If someone obtained a high mark on a test or in athletics, he was always pleased, since that meant that he would have to push himself higher, extend himself even further, which he loved.

So he never suspected me that winter; he never suspected that I wanted him to fail.

On the surface, all feelings had been locked up for the winter. All effort had been put into cold storage until spring. Examinations came and went, the Atlantis Charter members passed resolutions and put them into sluggish operation. Ahead next year was college, but we pretended that it didn't exist. It seemed far away yet, in some remote future. The ground was still and frozen; bare branches of trees twisted and rattled in the wind like dry bones; in the woods, the stems of the maidenhair fern were black and wilted and dead. And the students of Wilson seemed half-dead, too, their minds locked in the winter, staring out dumbly at fog and ice through hooded jackets.

Only Jonathan's mind moved briskly through the winter. It was as if the cold air sent more oxygen to his brain and he became sharper, turning out ideas in an uninterrupted flow. Bleakly I watched him triumph over German and calculus, and waited for him to fall.

Then one day he helped Arthur Langley cheat on a test. I sat in class, my mind whirling. All that blather about Atlantis and doing one's best! All that blather—and here he was cheating like anyone else. Allowing Arthur Langley to copy his paper.

If I hadn't seen it with my own eyes, I wouldn't have believed it. As it was, I half believed it was a mirage, an aberration of my mind. Jonathan. Not that I believed anyone was perfect. How well I knew how easy it is to break some rule, without thinking. Hadn't I blithely lied and skipped class only a few weeks ago?

But *cheating*. It was an act that didn't seem consistent with Jonathan's character. Had I never known him at all? I looked at his face, framed in dark hair, as he bent over a table. Was Atlantis only a pretense? My mind spun. If Casey found out, the punishment would be an automatic *F* for the test. Even if his other average for the year was an *A*, she would drop him to a *C* for a final grade. And there would go any chance for Jonathan to be in the running for valedictorian or salutatorian honors, I thought. Akins and Connie Desmond would capture those coveted academic prizes.

I realized that I was staring. Jonathan looked up and stared back at me, startled, caught off guard, conscious now of

53

being observed. A dull flush spread upward from his collar line. Oh, he was guilty. He was guilty, all right.

He wasn't going to get away with it. Anger and indignation swept over me, the desire to expose him. Then the feeling changed, swerving in another direction. Lose class honors, I thought sickly. I looked out the window. Horsetail clouds lay in a string across a blue sky. Somewhere over town a kite tail rose in the sky, then plummeted to earth. I wouldn't tell, I realized. I wouldn't say anything at all. It would never be mentioned.

Saturday Jonathan came over to work on the paper. His mind wasn't on it, and later I won two straight games of cribbage. He pushed the cribbage board away finally.

"I guess I'm not in the mood for playing."

"I've got a new record. Want to hear it?"

"Let's just skip it today, huh?"

He looked miserable, unhappy, almost ill. His face, usually animated and alert, looked gray and tired. There were black hollows under his eyes, as if he hadn't slept all night, and under my scrutiny, his mouth twisted despairingly.

"Okay, I did it," he said defiantly.

"Did what?" My voice came out in a strange croak, and I laughed hoarsely. I knew what he was talking about. I knew all right. We both knew. We hadn't thought of anything else since it happened.

Jonathan spread his hands outward in a helpless gesture. The palm of his left hand was exposed with the movement and I stared at it. Then my glance skidded away. My tongue ran nervously over my lips, which were suddenly dry and parched.

Jonathan jerked to his feet and looked wildly around the room, as if there, in the soft worn cushions of the davenport or chairs, or in the bookshelves lined with books, he might see some hiding place.

"You know," he said bitterly.

"I don't know what you're talking about," I cried. "Honestly, you act like some madman, jumping up, saying you did something—and I don't know what you're talking about!" I laughed hoarsely again. "You might at least tell me what you're talking about, for crying out loud."

"The test."

"Test?" I said blankly. It was strange. There in the room, hearing my own words, I didn't believe it had happened. It was something that never had happened. I was prepared to stake my life on it.

Jonathan's mouth twisted again. I saw the conflict in his face, the terrible agony of indecision. Then his face grew calm and stoic.

"You don't have to lie for me, Ann," he said flatly.

I stared at him and didn't answer.

He was suddenly composed, the Jonathan I knew. "In Atlantis one doesn't lie, remember?"

I swallowed.

"You saw Langley, didn't you?" he said.

I nodded miserably.

"I don't know what made me do it." The tone of his voice was incredulous, as if the aberration surprised him as much as me, as if he couldn't believe it even yet. "Suddenly the test was there, and I knew he wasn't prepared, so I slid it over." He straightened as if bracing himself. "I won't be playing in the game Friday. That's out now."

"Jonathan—" I began, making a move toward him.

"It's out of the question," he said sharply, cutting me off. "I wouldn't consider going now."

"What about the team?"

"Akins will take my place."

I wasn't going to mention Casey, but Jonathan had thought of that, too. "Casey will drop me to an *F* on the final grade," he said. "That means either Connie or Akins will get valedictorian."

"I'm sorry."

"It isn't important," Jonathan said. "Atlantis—" He didn't finish the sentence. I knew what he had meant to say. The whole year was bound up in the idea of Atlantis. Winning one of the class's academic honors was important, but it was the ideal of Atlantis that had captured his imagination.

"I'll have to tell the coach," Jonathan said. "He'd probably like to know today if I can catch him. Want to walk down to school?"

It was the last thing in the world I wanted to do. I put on my jacket and, without protest, followed him out of the house.

At Wilson a half dozen fellows were sprinting, keeping in shape by taking a couple of turns around the track. They weren't running hard, simply jogging in a lazy, methodical way, yelling to each other once in a while. Two girls leaned on the fence watching them, and their voices rose in the air, too—sweet, light voices, calling encouragement.

The coach was standing at the edge of the sand jumping pit. He wore an athletic jacket with a big W on the breast and a baseball cap. His name was Hopkins; he was young, fairly new at Wilson, happy to have a winning basketball team.

He looked up and smiled. "Hello, Jonathan," he said, including me in the glance, too. Nobody was vaulting today or shot-putting or throwing the javelin; all that equipment was locked up in the dark recesses of the building for the winter.

"I won't be playing in the game Friday," Jonathan said. "You better plan on someone taking my place on the team."

"Hey, don't tell me that," Hopkins said. "I'm planning for us to beat Kennedy Friday." He always spoke in a friendly, joking way to the boys; he wasn't alarmed even now. He was smiling and relaxed, half joking.

"I'm sorry—I won't be going," Jonathan said stiffly. His face was strained and white again.

"I hope you aren't serious," Hopkins said, sobering. "What's the trouble?"

"I broke one of the rules of Atlantis."

Hopkins smiled. "So?"

"So—I won't be going," Jonathan said in a low voice.

Hopkins had heard of Atlantis. All the teachers at Wilson were aware of it. Perhaps he had even seen the Atlantis Charter, that elaborate scroll that hung on the wall of the Journalism Room. But he dismissed it now, as he dismissed all things that didn't coincide with athletics.

"Well . . ." he said, and smiled indulgently, prepared to overlook the breaking of a rule in some other department that wasn't his own. "I don't think anything can be so bad that—"

"I let someone copy my test," Jonathan said.

The coach looked startled and gave him his full attention now. Cheating on a test, outside his department, still carried grave school penalties. It was not something that could be ignored even by him. Now that it had been stated, it hung in the air, tangible, physical, like a blistered heel or a broken leg that had to be dealt with.

"I'm sorry to hear that," he said stiffly.

"Yes, sir," Jonathan said miserably.

"Whose class was it?"

"Casey's."

"We can't expect leniency there."

"I wasn't expecting any leniency," Jonathan said. "I'm prepared not to play Friday."

"I wish I could help you," Hopkins said. "Under the circumstances, I think we better scratch your name." He looked at Jonathan curiously, as if wondering what had possessed him to do it, then evidently decided against questioning, and dropped it.

"I'm sorry," he said, and looked out again at the track and at the runners jogging in their T-shirts.

We had been dismissed. Jonathan and I walked away from the field and down the street. The winter sunlight fell through the leaves and made cold splashes of pale yellow on the walk. Jonathan kicked a wilted stray leaf away with his foot and then slowly turned and crossed the street.

"Just as well see Casey, too."

I looked at him, startled. I didn't want to see Casey today. I didn't want to see Casey ever.

Now that he had decided, he seemed bent on getting it over with. I followed him, feeling dread tighten in my chest. I had never been inside Casey's house. Once on Halloween someone had suggested removing the gate from her fence, but in the end everyone had been too intimidated. It was an old house, made forbidding by the fact that Casey lived there. Actually, it was one of the typical-looking older houses of the town, not ancient or large enough to be distinctive, a medium-sized house that was simply old. Casey and Penny, both unmarried, lived there together and walked the three blocks to Wilson each morning with their black umbrellas held over their heads to fend off the rain. They knew everyone in town who had ever gone to Wilson and, except for Herrider, had never been seriously challenged in their absolute authority.

Jonathan's face grew whiter and more strained as we neared the house. I saw his glance skip over the windows, a sliding glance that sought a face. When we reached the gate his look was actually apprehensive and his step faltered and came to a stop.

Then some strength of fortitude sustained him; he took a deep breath, loped lightly up the steps, and turned the doorbell. It was a strange affair that you turned in the manner of winding a clock; a little jangling sound came from its inner parts, and the door opened.

Casey herself stood there, a ridiculous purple scarf tied around her head. It made her look like someone completely strange: a cleaning woman.

"May we come in?" Jonathan said.

"Yes—yes, of course." She seemed slightly flustered.

We walked into a formal-looking living room filled with old furniture and portraits. It wasn't a room for sitting, and we stood. I remember that very clearly, the three of us simply standing in the middle of the room.

"I wanted to tell you, Miss Casey," Jonathan said, "that I let someone copy my test yesterday."

It took a lot of courage to say those words. I could never have brought myself to say them—but then I didn't have Jonathan's moral fiber.

Casey looked surprised, then stern. Her glance swept over

Jonathan's face, prepared to ferret out truth, guile, ulterior motive. Years of working with students had given her a suspicious mind. Apparently satisifed that there was none, she nodded.

"All right. Thank you for telling me, Jonathan." She walked over to a desk on which an old-fashioned leather valise was sitting. She unbuckled the valise and found his test paper.

"I'm giving you an *F*," she said, and marked the paper. "You do not have to reveal the name. I'll find out myself."

Jonathan nodded. There didn't seem to be anything else to say, so we turned and walked out the door and out the gate, which closed with a definite, metallic clang, and then we were on the street again.

It was over. At least it was over. I thought that nothing more terrible could happen. About that I was wrong, too, but at the time, that was the stray thought that floated across my mind.

Everyone at Wilson, of course, knew on Monday that Jonathan had been suspended from the basketball team. It was all over school, a whisper that ran down the corridors and past the steel lockers. Everyone politely averted his eyes when Jonathan walked by. There was an uncomfortable silence when he came into a room, a sudden burst of activity that had nothing to do with him.

I thought that Jonathan looked the same. It was as if he said, "Nothing happened. Everything is the same as always. I am the same as I always was." But it was just a bluff. By noon his face was white and tense. He looked as if he had lost weight in the three hours. Someone spoke to him, and color shot into his face. Then in the middle of class he got up and left the room in a sort of staggering motion. And pity swept over me. He was like a king who had been deposed, stripped of his crown and robes, to reveal only a human being after all.

Tuesday he was quiet and subdued. Wednesday he took the initiative and came to school with his head shaved. I stared at him in disbelief.

"For crying out loud, what happened?" I felt the smile slide over my face. "Did you meet up with a scalping party, or what?" I waited for him to smile back.

"I thought it would be more comfortable," he said curtly.

The tone of his voice said that he didn't want to talk about it. I realized with a flash of insight that it was some self-imposed penance, like a monk's vow, that he had taken to punish himself for cheating (one of those things you know about another person that you know you will never mention).

"I like it. It looks real cool." We walked on down the hallway, through the journalism-class doorway.

The lack of hair gave him a strange bald look that made me want to burst out laughing. At the same time it sobered me as abruptly as a plunge into icy water. I would never have imposed a penalty on myself for any wrongdoing. My only concern would have been to get out of it as easily and quickly as possible. There was a kind of dignity about Jonathan's behavior that impressed me and, at the same time, made me feel that I had never known him. It ranked with Mahatma Ghandi's fasting or a Hindu's lying on a bed of nails.

Everyone in class turned and stared at Jonathan—showing the undisguised curiosity and amusement that accompanied anything that deviated from the ordinary at Wilson. I pulled out a piece of paper and began to work energetically, as if it were the most normal thing in the world to shave one's head and look like a monk. Quite normal.

"Now that we've all seen Jonathan's haircut," Penny said dryly, "shall we get back to getting out the paper?"

The class ended; students trailed out of the room. Jonathan stayed on to work on an editorial.

"Want to take a look at what I've got?"

"What? Oh, yeah, sure," I mumbled.

I looked numbly down at the paper on the desk, as if it were magnetized and I would never be able to look away. The room was silent as a funeral. The tension was unbearable. I had the wild urge to laugh, as I had once in English class when Casey had warned us that the Murder of Lidice was a very solemn subject, and when I, choking with laughter, had to leave the room and go out into the hallway, where I dissolved into loud guffaws at the thought of 190 Czechoslovakian men being murdered.

"I didn't write the editorial the first of the year because I thought maybe the war was old stuff now," Jonathan said. "Then today I thought about it again and I saw it applied just as much today as it did when the war was on."

The editorial was good, I think, very good, although today I can't remember a word of it. Still, I knew the thought of the Vietnam War continued to hold Jonathan, as did the prisoners of that war, whom he had been writing about.

"I'm nineteen years old," Jonathan said. "I could have been one of them myself. I wonder what I would have done."

I looked at him, trying to visualize him as a soldier in a war: Jonathan, helmeted, carrying a gun; Jonathan, a

P.O.W. tied up in some hut and being tortured by the enemy. My eyes squinted as I concentrated, but for the life of me I could not imagine Jonathan in any other role except the one he held now, leader of the senior class at Wilson.

"I couldn't have stood it," Jonathan said. "I would have broken."

I wanted to protest. Jonathan, broken? But even as disbelief washed through me, I felt that he had touched a partial truth. Jonathan wouldn't have been good in a war. He would have sat on the ground and wept. He would have forgotten that he was there to kill people. In the middle of a battle he would have started to tell people about a lost place called Atlantis.

"You would have done what the rest did," I said loyally.

"No, I would have broken," Jonathan said in a strange, sure voice.

We stared at each other across the room, which was filled with sunlight. Was it true? If he had been a prisoner of war, would he have broken? Yes, as thin vases of fine glass break, I thought, and shatter into a million pieces.

It was a moment in time that still has a strange hold on my mind. I can still see him even today, his head shaved—like a prisoner of war himself—and hear the strange quality of his voice when he spoke. I think it was in that moment, too, that I knew I loved him.

Why it should be that you should love someone more in a moment of human frailty than one of strength I don't know, but I believe it is true.

Five

Jonathan jogged on through the winter like a long-distance runner, picking up his weekly A's in German, writing his Atlantis column for the paper, playing basketball, winning at cribbage.

Nothing suited him better than to be absolutely swamped with work, dive in and clear it all away, and arrive at the door on Saturday night showered, his hair still damp, wearing a fresh white shirt.

"Done studying?" he would say with irritating innocence.

"Oh, yes—*certainly*," I would say with heavy sarcasm. Then he would grin, knowing all the time, of course, that I had barely started.

"Am I too early—do you have to work?" His eyebrows would lift, polite, innocent.

It was always understood in Jonathan's world that work

came before pleasure. In my own world, I reversed the procedure as much as possible, waiting until Sunday night to do most of my studying.

Two days before Christmas he stamped his feet on the doormat, shook the rain out of his hair, and followed me inside. In the rec room, he dumped a box of candy into my arms.

"I know how much these things mean to you," he said carelessly, and grinned again.

"They don't mean so much to me," I said firmly, denying it.

"You can have all the soft ones. I'll take the chewy ones."

It was the nearest thing to romance our relationship had achieved. He liked me best when he was teasing me about some deficiency. It amused him to see me squirm and fight back. Also, I think lightness and humor did not come easily to him, so he enjoyed the play of wits. It was a contest he was never sure of winning. Intellectually superior, he was not gifted with the quick tongue or easy remark. Also of course, it kept our relationship on exactly the level he wanted it: half serious, half bantering. I noted that too.

Any other boy by this time would have announced his undying love, or at least tried a couple of passes. It wasn't a normal relationship, I thought, looking at him critically as he chewed a chocolate. But of course, I didn't really believe that. It was the most normal relationship in the world. What could be more normal than Jonathan sitting beside me now carefully picking out all the chewy chocolates in the box, pointing out that you could tell which was which by the markings on top.

"Just remembered—got some news," Jonathan mumbled.

"What?"

"Herrider is resigning."

"You've got to be kidding."

"No, it's true. The school board's already been notified."

Herrider had never really liked Wilson, and he had never liked Jonathan. We had never liked him either, so we looked at each other now and grinned wickedly.

I suppose actually Herrider quit for personal reasons, but to Jonathan, of course, it was another victory for Atlantis; an example that proved that right triumphs in the world.

Right always triumphed in Jonathan's mind. He saw it rather globally: a giant battleground where right and wrong fought and right won. The United States had won World War II because it was right. The North had won the Civil War instead of the South because it was right. You always won an argument if you were right. You always won in sports if you were right. This had no logic, and wasn't even true, but in Jonathan's mind it was true, and it was the measuring stick from which all of his actions stemmed.

Right always triumphed. The first weekend of January he spent endless hours of time marshaling volunteer troops to ring doorbells and collect piles of newspapers and Coke cans for a family whose house had burned down the last night of December. He did not know the family himself, but obviously it was an area where evil had temporarily won in the world, so all of his energy was expended on making right triumph.

I padded along behind Carol Marshall one cold frosty day, feeling like a fool, ringing doorbells, digging in garbage sacks.

"Is that all we've got?" Jonathan said at noon, looking

around him at the playground, which was littered with little piles of plastic bags and stacks of newspapers. "I mean—is this *all*?"

Up to this point we had thought we had done fairly well. Jonathan shamed us with his voice; we saw ourselves small and selfish, devoid of proper humanitarian instincts.

"How much do you think we should get?" Akins said uncertainly.

"Why, at least up to here," Jonathan said, making a mark even with his chest. "The baseball diamond should be covered, don't you think? I mean—if we're representing Wilson," he said, his voice trailing off apologetically. Representing Wilson was another kind of sacred law with him.

Coster immediately agreed that we should get that much. "At *least*," he said, glaring at the rest of us.

"Yes," Akins said. "We should—"

We trooped out into the cold again, this time staying out for six hours, amassing a huge mountain of the recyclable cans and newspapers, which we stared at with faint astonishment in the dimming twilight of a winter day.

Wilson that year, under the leadership of Jonathan, used its collective energy to feed the poor of Africa, send the soccer team to Canada, and donate a thousand dollars to UGN. Volunteer groups sang and put on skits for nursing homes; fifty students learned mouth-to-mouth resuscitation at the fire department; I believe at least a dozen students learned the sign language of the deaf.

Three hundred dollars was also collected to help send a boy to South America for the summer to be a student missionary, a personal project of Jonathan's. It had nothing to do with Wilson, but seemed like the kind of thing a person should do, as Jonathan put it, and therefore, it should be encouraged and sponsored. Jonathan himself did not believe in God. Aiming at the highest was a kind of religion with him, however; in sports, in grades, and in ethics.

All of this was not accomplished effortlessly, without grumbling or resentment. Coster and Akins, natural rivals of Jonathan, went along often only if an idea could be presented as their own. It was natural at our age to do as little as possible, to be as selfish and lazy as possible, so at the end of February, when winter finally came and the ground froze in earnest, there was a lull in activity, a lowering of spirits and will.

I kept up a running commentary of protest all through the winter, which Jonathan ignored.

"It isn't *normal* to study all of the time," I protested one night.

Jonathan grinned. "You kill me, Ann," he said. "You really kill me."

"It isn't *natural*."

He threw back his head and laughed.

"What good are all these A's going to do me?"

A small smile started at the corner of Jonathan's mouth. "You never know. You might need them."

"I mean—really."

"If you're going to college you'll need them."

"I doubt if I'll go."

"What's really eating you?"

"Arthur Langley asked me to go to the game with him Friday night," I said, letting my breath out.

"Oh?" He said it carefully, without any emotion in his voice. "You going?"

"I haven't decided. I told him I'd let him know Tuesday."

"I don't see any reason why you shouldn't go," Jonathan said indifferently, shrugging. "I mean, if you want to. I have to play."

It didn't seem loyal, and yet he had no hold on me. I remembered suddenly, too, how it had been in the summer, drifting through the days waiting for a boy to call, driving someplace carelessly in the summer twilight, the next day repeating the experience with a different boy. A sudden longing swept over me for the fickleness of that time.

"Maybe I will go. If you don't mind."

"Why would I mind?" Jonathan said, looking at me curiously.

I stared at him.

"I don't know—I thought—" I mumbled, and turned away in confusion.

I had thought, of course, that he would be jealous. I had thought that our relationship was special to him, too.

I didn't go to the game with Arthur Langley. I don't think I had ever intended to go really. Jonathan was there to jog the next morning the same as usual.

"Better get some extra study in this evening," he puffed as we jogged along.

I nodded meekly. I had been goofing off. Last week I had done nothing and had dropped to a C.

"One thing about a language. Got to do it every day."

Jonathan had given up his idea of my being one of Wilson's great women track stars. "You don't seem to have the competitive genes—I mean, not enough to be really good. Maybe you'd better stick to studying," he said one day.

We took another turn around the block, past stately white houses that looked out at the street in sleepy, snobbish grandeur, past a new development, past a new apartment house.

"You've really done quite well."

"Thanks." I felt awkward at the unaccustomed compliment. Despite a pretense that I couldn't care less, I had worked hard.

"Quite well—considering."

"Considering! Considering what?" I said sarcastically.

"You didn't really want to go to the game with Langley, did you?" Jonathan said, switching the subject, peering at my face closely.

He continued to jog in a steady, methodical way. "I didn't think you did. You're much happier this year. It's because you're studying more," he said matter-of-factly. "I'm good for you that way."

I had the feeling again of a doctor-patient relationship. It wasn't a feeling I particularly liked. I was used to boys telling me they loved me. A vague wisp of disappointment trailed through me, then evaporated like fog. Even though he wasn't demonstrative, I never doubted Jonathan's affection for me.

No one was ever clumsier or less adept at building things than Jonathan, and no one ever enjoyed it more. That winter, with the enthusiasm of the complete amateur, he built kites and stilts and skateboards. The kites crashed to earth, the stilts broke, the wheels came off the skateboards. He cheerfully rebuilt them and improvised new models. Having no brothers, he never stopped to think that they were the pleasures of younger boys; he would have been hurt if anyone had suggested they weren't safe; and none of us dared tell him that we didn't want to try them. His pleasure was too innocent. And I understood too that it was his way of showing affection. He could not say openly words like love. It wasn't in his character to hold hands in the hall; he built kites and stilts.

When he tried the stilts on, he leaned against the house, pushed his two feet into the straps, and shoved off like a gangly stork. He towered above me like a giant. I had the strange sensation, looking up, that Jonathan had grown in the night and become part of a different race, some race that was vastly superior physically and intellectually. He stood so far above me that I could never reach him. I felt a moment of panic. Even if I studied night and day I could never catch up with Jonathan. I had wasted too many years. I was too frivolous. One day he would look at me silently, regretfully; then he would turn his back and go on alone.

"Come on. Try it." He grinned.

I put my feet into the straps. Then, almost as tall as he, I clumped around the yard with him as relief swept through me.

We ended up eventually at the playground at Wilson. No matter where we went that winter, we always took a route home that went by Wilson. It was as if it were some touchstone for Jonathan, the physical core of his being that kept him in tune with the world. There was someone always in the playing field, a band practicing marching or just individuals playing a game of touch tackle or flying kites or model airplanes. Jonathan would lean against the fence and watch them silently. I never knew what he was thinking in those moments because he never spoke, and after a few minutes, satisfied, he would move on.

Jonathan always had followers. Pretty soon there were a

71

half dozen others walking with stilts around the playground. We spent the whole afternoon there, a curious afternoon when we walked tall like storks over a familiar playground, the town shrunken, pedestrians and cars like toys, diminished. Afterward we ate a hamburger downtown, played some records in a jukebox, and talked to Coster and Akins, who usually drifted in. It was night, a clear night with a large, orange, unreal moon, when we finally started for home on our stilts.

Jonathan and I trod silently through the school yard at Wilson, and the school sank into me. I caught something of the feeling that I think Jonathan always felt. I had such a strong feeling of belonging to Wilson and to its traditions that the surroundings seemed to sink into me and become part of me. The brick building that had been built in 1918, the maples, all covered by soft moonlight.

Our shadows stretched out in the pale light, gigantic extensions of ourselves, gigantic possibilities that we had never dreamed or intended or thought possible. It was as if in the past year we had grown beyond ourselves and become more than had ever been intended.

And now, in the dreamlike night, pain caught at my throat. It must be the way great athletes feel when they leave a college where they have excelled. The ordinary world can never again provide that same feeling of brilliance and reality as that time when they caught dazzling passes on a green field—those moments of singular triumph—and so all through their life they live over and over again that one moment in time and history.

"In Atlantis . . ." It was a phrase that fell from the lips of even Coster and Akins now. I often heard it as I moved down a hallway, my ears snatching it from the rubble of sound, and smiled to myself. Even the scoffers and dissenters had succumbed finally to its insidious spell. Lawlessness had been vanquished; in its place, there was the fumbling desire to somehow rise above one's true and selfish nature and be something better.

The only snowfall of the year was a sudden flurry that came the following week, a halfhearted showering of white down on shoulders and trees. It started as a few sluggish white flakes mixed with rain that gathered heavily at the edge of windshield wipers, then melted and trailed down the glass like bitter, reluctant tears. By school time the next morning it had managed to cover the grounds and sidewalks of Wilson and the limbs of the maple trees overhead.

When I reached school a group of boys had packed snowballs, half covered with dirt, and were sailing them at girls as they came up the walk. They responded with shrieks, and ducked into the building.

Suddenly a familiar figure came up the walk—Raymond Summers, wearing a stocking cap and glasses. The group enthusiastically turned as one and began to pelt him mercilessly with snowballs. It was difficult in a public school not to pick on someone like Raymond Summers. His timidity and aversion to physical contact seemed to invite teasing and heckling.

"Hey—wait. Please. My clothes!" he protested as he shrank away from the onslaught. "Please. Don't—" his voice whined. "My glasses!" he pleaded, his hands going up over his face to protect them.

His tormenters came forward, sailing the dirty snowballs

into his face. Jonathan, standing on the steps, removed from the action, watching, suddenly stepped in. Leaning down, he swiftly scooped up the fresh snow into several balls and shot them in the direction of the gang of boys.

Grinning, they turned away from Raymond Summers and fell upon him with a cheerful vengence. Raymond Summers scuttled up the steps and into the safety of the building. Jonathan, overwhelmed by the pack, lay on his back in the snow. Someone was cramming snow down his neck. He energetically put his knee into Coster's stomach. Coster yelled and then retaliated by smearing Jonathan's face with snow. Langley was perched on his right leg, firmly pinning it to the ground.

A bell rang, and it was all over as swiftly as it had started. The boys dispersed, and Jonathan, still brushing snow off his clothes, limped up the steps and into the building. He leaned against his locker, breathing heavily. There was a cut on his cheek where a dirty snowball had scraped; he looked exhausted.

"You all right?" I said, peering at his face.

"Yeah. Be okay—in a minute," he gasped. He rubbed the dirt off his face with a towel, then leaned against the locker, a strange look in his eyes.

He looked like Jesus of Nazareth after being stoned by the mob. It was as if, there in a swift, savage, snow-covered moment, he had become the enemy. Forgetting that he was the leader of the school, they had turned, as a mob, to vanquish him. Something of that knowledge was in his face as he leaned against the locker, with a surprised, stunned look. Then he shrugged it off.

"Okay now," he said, "Ready for class." And he calmly

joined me as if nothing had happened. He never mentioned it again, and by evening the snow had melted.

All the time spring was coming. One day in March I woke up just before dawn, and the air was filled with the sound of birds chattering. I had not missed them or even thought about them. Now, hearing them, I realized they'd been gone all winter! Now they'd come back and it was spring.

Jonathan seemed to gather some new energy with spring. His figure bounded down the halls of Wilson, organizing, marshaling. His nimble mind turned out columns and sports stories; his thin body vaulted into the air on the end of a slender pole, sank down into foam padding.

Still, he seemed restless and dissatisfied, as if he hadn't achieved enough, as if somehow, with spring, Atlantis was getting away from him. That was partly true. With spring, suddenly the idea that had held us in the winter now seemed as restricting as a straitjacket. By May nobody wanted anymore to be perfect; everyone wanted to skip school and break the rules.

I could not study those days. I sat on the patio, and the warmth of the sun sank into me and slowed my blood. As I lay on the concrete one afternoon the first part of June, my arms outstretched, I caught the scent of blossoms and flowers, and I stared through the sunlight, drugged. School would be over in two weeks.

I was not in the running for school honors, of course. I had started too late. For the year, I had done surprisingly well. Under Jonathan's prodding I had managed a credible A–B average. Since I had started so low, I was in the race for The Most Improved Student. There was a plaque given each year to this student—not one of the major prizes of the school—but still, it occurred to me that I might get it if I did well on my finals.

Just the same, I didn't move. I lay in the sunlight, pinned like a moth to the warm concrete, smelling the fragrance of spring, held by inertia. It was as if my true shallow nature had finally caught up with me. I lay there all weekend.

"Aren't you going to study?" Mother asked, peering down at my face.

"No."

Nevertheless, I felt a sense of something like shock when the week of the finals came and I wasn't prepared. I had hardly studied at all. I went into my German test desperately muttering vocabulary. By the end of the day, when the last final came, my shoulders drooped with defeat.

"You'll do all right," Jonathan said, shooting a quick look at my face.

I stared at him bleakly. His face looked strange, like someone I didn't know. I had never known him. He had always been superior, someone so far ahead of me that now it seemed incredible that he had ever bothered with me.

I flunked the test. I knew I would. And Jonathan did not get class honors because of the *F* Casey had given him. He ended up third in the class. I looked at him as we walked out of assembly where the awards had been announced, but he seemed relieved to know. With the decision announced, he immediately turned back into his old self. Losses did not really bother him, I realized, if he thought he had done the right thing.

"Does Martha's Peak really have snow on it the year around?" he asked. Martha's Peak was the place chosen for the Senior Class Picnic.

"Most years."

Jonathan's face grew thoughtful. "You could make something in the snow and it would never melt," he said.

"I suppose it would melt sometime," I said vaguely. "Or someone might knock it down."

"But if they didn't—" Jonathan persisted. "If nobody knocked it down, it could stay there for months—years."

I stared at him. I didn't know what he was driving at.

"We could build something there. The whole class. It could stay there for years," Jonathan said enthusiastically. "Wouldn't that be great?"

I hadn't thought about it, so I didn't know whether it would be great or not. I imagined a giant snowball rolled up in the snow on top of Martha's Peak. But what was so great about that? I must have looked blank.

"A snow sculpture," Jonathan said. "Something big. Lincoln. Or a Greek. Yeah," he said. "A Greek statue. Someone in the art class could do it."

I stared at him. I thought he was probably crazy. Here he had lost class honors and he was happily contemplating making a statue in the snow that would last forever on Martha's Peak. If he was crazy, it was a wonderful kind of craziness.

"Something big," I said, grinning. "Something that would last a million years."

When we got to Martha's Peak the day of the Senior Class Picnic, nobody could remember what Greeks looked like, and Jonathan's project threatened to disintegrate completely into chaos. One segment of students in the class had enterprisingly built a snow fort, and now, barricaded behind it, they energetically began to bombard the rest of us with snowballs. It was the first real snow most of the class had seen all year. Boys swerved away, tumbling in the whiteness, pelting each other. Girls screamed and boys forced snow down their necks. In a shelter, teachers laid out food on tables.

Jonathan stood in the middle of another group unsuccessfully trying to get the snow sculpture off the ground. It was a day dedicated to fun. No one really wanted to expend the energy on serious projects. Who cared about the Greeks anyway? This was America.

"We could make something that might last a year," Jonathan said desperately. He looked at Akins for help, then Langley, but Langley, still angry about being turned in for cheating, turned away coldly.

Only Raymond Summers seemed interested. "I think I could do it if I had a picture to go by," he said.

"All right," Jonathan said crisply. "You'll be the one to do it. The rest of us will make the base and the rough outline. You can sculpt it."

Somehow the project got started. One of the boys who had a car drove back to town and found a picture and brought back some tools. Akins and Coster began engineering the making of blocks that would stack on top of each other. By lunchtime others joined the act, and a clumsy structure began to rise into the air. By two o'clock it had begun to have the look of something large and permanent, and a half hour later, Raymond Summers began the work of creating it into a sculpture of a Greek.

Jonathan, standing looking up, was supervising the project. The sun shone down on his face, and, suddenly hot, he took off his jacket. Akins was on his knees in the snow, slowly and carefully carving "Atlantis 77" on the base of the statue.

The day dwindled away and the sun left the peak. Part of the class left; then gradually others straggled away until at the end there were only a couple dozen of the dedicated remaining. We stood in a ring around the statue eating hot dogs, handing up snow, and shouting encouragement to Raymond Summers.

In his glory, Raymond gravely carved a nose on the face, then scooped out a chin, then the top of the head, very carefully putting in the Greek details, the olive wreath, the toga.

"That looks great," Jonathan said. "That really looks great, Raymond."

Who could deny it? Even if it was Raymond. It really did look great, and it was a grand day, a perfect day to end the year.

I do not know if the class statue of Atlantis is still standing on Martha's Peak now or not. I would like to think that it will stand there forever, on that peak where snow does not melt from the top all year, permanent and immortal, as Jonathan conceived it in his mind, but reason tells me that it is probably gone, melted or knocked down by snowballs, or swept away by a careless snowplow.

I like to think that it is still there, like that plaque in a trophy case with Jonathan's name on it, that scroll on a wall, and an editorial buried in an old Wilson newspaper file about prisoners of war. Time or death cannot erase the really important things, can it?

Six

S ometimes, waking on those summer mornings that
followed, my joy was so complete that I felt like
shouting. Other times I resented Jonathan with a
bitterness that was almost hate. His rules were the bars of a
prison that held me caged.

Everyone else had succumbed to the forbidden pleasures of
summer. Cars rode wildly through the long summer nights;
there were beach parties, drinking, music, and the smoking
of forbidden weeds. I longed for Jonathan to commit some
wild improbable sin, to throw away his rules for the summer,
say madly that he loved me. He never did, of course.

On this day we lay on the Soldug riverbank exhausted
from swinging out on the ring over the river. My body was
white and shriveled from diving into the cool water, and
Jonathan, who, incredibly, had never learned to swim, lay
watching me idly.

"You really dig this, don't you?" he said.

"Dig what?"

"The sun, the water."

I smiled and didn't answer.

"You're pretty like this," Jonathan said. He looked at me critically. "If you lost ten pounds you'd be a real knockout."

"If I lost ten pounds," I said coldly.

"Hey, don't get mad."

"I'm not mad."

"You're fine the way you are."

"But I'd be better ten pounds lighter," I insisted.

"You're like your mother. You have a tendency to be a little chunky. When you get older, you'll probably have to watch it. That's all I meant," he said apologetically.

When *you* get older, *you*'ll have to watch it, too, I thought. I know your weakness, Jonathan. You like boys. The thought popped into my head and exploded like a series of firecrackers. I felt sick, physically ill as if I were going to vomit. You like boys a little too much, I thought. You have a tendency to be a little queer, a little faggish, a little effeminate. When you get older, you'll probably have to watch it, I thought coldly.

That's a lie, a dirty lie! something in my brain shouted. He's just as normal as any boy.

Is he? Is he? another part shouted. My hand squeezed the sand into a hard ball. There rose in my mind, damning as a Polaroid print, an image of Jonathan coming down the hall, his arm lightly flung over another boy's. Why else hadn't he told me he loved me?

"You're a little abnormal yourself," I said, smiling sickly, and I trickled the sand lightly over his stomach. It kept me

81

busy, so I didn't have to look at him. I knew the truth about him. I had always known the truth about him.

"Time to go home," Jonathan said, springing up.

After that I began to watch him, not really consciously, but rather on a deep level of my mind that stayed apart from the rest of me. He would make a mistake and then he would fall, that Jonathan the Perfect who reached for some invisible high mark. He would make a mistake and I would let him know that I knew, that I, Ann Taylor, was not fooled, had never been fooled. I would let him know that I did not at all appreciate his deceit, his treachery.

On other days I was sane and knew that Jonathan was perfectly normal, a special, unique individual who had created a world called Atlantis. At twelve, just after lunch, he would call me, and we would bicycle down to the Soldug River and spend the afternoon swimming and lying on the bank. His hand would reach out awkwardly and touch mine, and I would feel a wild, impossible joy rise in my throat.

One day in July Jonathan appeared at the door rolling a huge inner tube; two homemade paddles were slung over his shoulder. He was wearing cutoffs, a floppy hat, and tennis shoes. He looked like a demented scarecrow.

"What is *that?*" I said. The inner tube was almost as high as my shoulders.

"Our new boat. Got it at the Dairy." He grinned and took a map out of his pocket. "I thought we'd go down the Soldug and explore a little and shoot some rapids."

"On that?"

"I figured it out mathematically. It should hold us both up. You sit on one side; I sit on the other. We paddle with the oars."

The Soldug narrows from the point of the swimming hole, growing more shallow and also, at points, more rapid. Splashing along in the water, having just fallen off, Jonathan threw himself on the side of the inner tube in a precarious balancing act and began paddling furiously.

"Indians around the corner," he gasped. "Just saw some scouts. Don't talk. Keep close to shore, and we'll try to sneak by them."

"You're craz——"

"Shh! Scalping party—must be a dozen of them. Keep your voice down."

He was paddling furiously toward shore, and now the inner tube began to glide along the shoreline. I had the strange impression suddenly that the scene was real. I glanced up to the bank, half expecting to see a brown face behind a tree.

Finally Jonathan stopped paddling and let the inner tube drift.

"Close," he said.

I smiled and looked at him. "You can't be real."

"Didn't you see them?" he said in an astonished voice.

I scooped some water in my hand and splashed it over his legs and he yelled.

"Let's try the rapids," I said with a grin.

"Here. Let me get my camera. I'll shoot as we go down."

The film Jonathan took that day looks like a seasick sailor's impression of the ocean. A streak of blue sky, then, as the camera bounced up and down, a crazy shot of the river and white rapids, and then another lopsided streak of shoreline blending with blue sky.

There is also a shot of me sitting inside the inner tube,

rolling like a wheel down a slight incline. I have a white canvas hat on my head, my legs are suntanned and bare, and I have red-white-and-blue canvas shoes on. I look utterly drenched, my shorts and blouse sag with water, and there is an expression of unadulterated happiness on my face.

By August the class was drifting away. Once it had been a fierce, tightly knit unit with officers and sharply defined cliques. Now, with fall coming, as if by some signal, it began to disperse. Some got married, some went to work, others impulsively joined a branch of the service. Even the class officers, the acknowledged leaders of the class, the defenders of Atlantis, seemed to lose interest in the game. They took vacations, had pot parties, and then, in the middle of August, sobered and began to pack their bags for college.

Jonathan and I were the only ones who were still held by the memory of Atlantis. It was as if it had been a game, and now everyone else had rushed on to some new diversion.

"You and I, friend. We're the only ones left," Jonathan said one day, looking gloomily at the empty rope swing that hung over the river. "Everyone else has gone."

"Yeah."

"You going to college this fall?"

"I've saved some money. I may." I dug a line in the sand with a stick. "What about you? Are you going to the U?"

"Maybe. I haven't decided yet," Jonathan said. "Mother doesn't know what she's going to do. Maybe I'll just bum around a year." He seemed restless, pulled by the end of summer.

"I hope you'll at least send me a postcard," I said bleakly.

"Oh, we'll write to you."

84

"We?"

Color shot into Jonathan's face. "Raymond and I."

"Raymond Summers?"

"Yes. He's got this idea of going down to Mexico," Jonathan said sheepishly.

"You're going to Mexico with Raymond Summers?" I said in a shocked voice. I felt Atlantis crumbling like a mud sand castle engulfed by the waves of a tide.

"What's wrong with Raymond?"

"Raymond Summers is not a normal person," I said flatly.

Jonathan looked at me, then threw back his head and laughed, with a howl that welled up from the pit of his stomach. "Ann! You kill me."

"He's gay."

"He's what?"

"You heard me."

"That's a lie," Jonathan said, giving me his full attention now.

"If you go with him, I never want to see you again."

"That sounds like a threat."

"Take it any way you like," I said sullenly.

"He's a perfectly normal boy," Jonathan said stoutly.

"I don't think so."

"I do."

"That's your choice."

Jonathan had been sitting; now he stood up with a jerk. "I think I will go with him. And I bet we have a swell time," he said defiantly. "A swell, normal time—without girls!"

"Then I'll say good-bye now."

Something in Jonathan's face faltered, then stiffened into remoteness.

"Good-bye," he said in a limp, indifferent voice.

He picked up his bicycle, threw one long leg over the seat, and pedaled stubbornly away, his hair standing up in odd little tufts on the back of his head.

On Wednesday Jonathan went out with Carmen Matia. Retaliating swiftly, I conspicuously drove around town for two days with Arthur Langley in his new convertible.

On Friday night I miserably joined a group of other girls at Carol Marshall's slumber party and sat in her rec room drinking Coke and eating potato chips.

Bored, we stared at TV.

"Anybody got any ideas what to do?" Carol said.

"Why don't we just drive around?" one of the other girls suggested.

"Wanna?" Carol asked the rest of us.

"Might as well."

We rose limply, and all piled into Carol's car.

Nobody was downtown. The streets held only middle-aged couples coming out of the Rialto Theatre, and some yelling, jostling freshman boys in front of the new ice-cream place that had opened for the summer.

"We could go up on Rocky Point and turn the spotlight on the neckers," I said. "They ought to be coming in now."

"Yeah, that would be a dirty trick," Carol said.

At twelve we decided that it was not only dirty; it was perfect. We turned the car in the direction of Rocky Point, found the opportune parking spot, and waited.

Shortly after twelve they started coming in. In the darkness it was hard to distinguish individual cars or see who was driving. I thought I saw Jack Coster. It seemed like a great idea to catch him in an embarrassing moment, so I whispered to Carol, "That blue car over there. Coster."

Carol nodded. "We'll give them a few minutes; then we'll give them the spotlight," she whispered. The other girls in the car giggled.

It was cold waiting in the car, and my teeth began to chatter. "We better hurry up. We're going to freeze to death."

Carol focused the spotlight and turned it on. I blinked as the bright light flooded the black sky; then I saw something I would have given most anything not to see.

"Jonathan," I whispered.

For a long time nothing happened at all. Nothing. Nobody moved. The yellow light shone through the darkness. From somewhere in the blackness laughter rang out, a sound that seemed to burst out of the night with unnatural loudness. Then the light abruptly snapped off. Like something in slow motion, the car turned around.

Carol gunned the motor, and we slowly descended Rocky Point Hill. I hadn't moved. I was still sitting stiffly upright, gripping the back of the front seat, a shocked expression on my face.

"I'm sorry, Ann," Carol stammered in my left ear. "I didn't know—"

I stared at her. I felt sick inside. "Please, do you mind? Just drop me off at home."

At home I crawled into bed and covered up my head with the covers. Jonathan and Carmen. In my mind it seemed as if the floodlight were still shining on them, that it would shine forever on the two figures scrambling for their clothes.

I never wanted tomorrow to come. I never wanted to face

Jonathan again. The whole thing seemed childish now and somehow cruel, an aspect of it I hadn't thought of before. When Jonathan found out I had been in on it, he would think it was juvenile, too. I didn't dare let my thoughts go any further. I could hear my heart pounding—*thump-thump*—like an overloaded washer. I had the terrible thought, half fear, half hope, that in the night it might burst through the thin wall that held it.

The following afternoon I bumped into Jonathan accidentally, coming out of Pete's. He looked startled.

"Oh, hello, Ann." An uncomfortable smile spread over his face.

I made an unintelligible sound in my throat.

"Been meaning to call you," he mumbled. "Going home?"

Our glances slid away from each other. Then we started walking down the street together. Suddenly we were both furiously walking in the direction of Wilson, not speaking, simply walking faster and faster, both of us remembering now what the other had done to him, our respective anger picking up speed as we walked.

"Look—Jonathan—about last night," I stammered.

Jonathan's eyes looked at me, two brown stones.

"I know you weren't in on it, Ann," he said. "You don't have to explain."

"Jonathan, please, listen—"

"You weren't there." His voice was clipped and curt. "I know that. I'm grateful for that."

Why did he keep lying to himself, hurting himself? He had looked squarely at me, hadn't he? I had seen comprehension and shock spread over his face. Or had I been wrong? Perhaps he hadn't really seen me, I thought cautiously. Blinded by the light, maybe he had seen only the dim outlines of a mass of jeering faces. Maybe the individual faces hadn't really registered in his brain. I felt heavy and burdened with guilt, like an old woman hunched over and broken with grief, like old Jessie Turner, who walked around town bent over, her back broken from picking cotton.

"I was there with Carol. I suggested it," I said.

"You what?" Jonathan said coldly.

I was afraid of his face. I couldn't stand lying. "You know and I know it was me. I was the one—"

Jonathan looked straight ahead of him. He didn't speak for so long I thought he would never speak.

"I knew it was you, Ann," he said quietly.

"Then why—?" My head spun.

"I didn't want it to be you. Do you understand? I didn't want it to be you," Jonathan said fiercely.

I nodded. Pain was coming into my throat.

"But I knew all the time it was. You were jealous. I hurt you. So in a way it was my fault," Jonathan said generously. "And I—I forgive you."

I swallowed and looked away.

"Thanks for telling me, and I forgive you," Jonathan said.

We walked down the street, stopping at the Wilson playground. Jonathan leaned against the fence, his glance following two boys who were running around the track. He put his hands in his pockets. In a flat, unemotional voice he said, "I'm having a party tonight. I'd like you to come."

"What kind of party?" I looked at him suspiciously.

"At my house. The school gang. Sort of a farewell."

"I might have something else to do," I hedged.

"I've invited everyone. I'd really like you to come."

"I'll try. What time?"

"Eight."

There was a long silence.

"I'm sorry about Carmen," Jonathan said.

I nodded. *It was my fault.* The words formed in my mind, but no words came out of my throat.

Seven

Everyone was at Jonathan's party. It was perhaps the party of the year, because few people had ever been invited to his home before. Most of them knew the old Merritt house where he lived, but it wasn't a place where you just dropped in casually, unannounced. How Jonathan's mother ever came to choose the house, I don't know, but there they were, the two of them in that grand old place that looked like a miniature castle.

The entire house was filled with light when I walked up the steps that night. It was like arriving at a magnificent ball, slightly late, with the sound of music floating from every window.

Jonathan, at the door in white shirt and slacks, looked like Jonathan, only a more happy and excited Jonathan than the usual one. It occurred to me that he must have been a lonely boy who had had few parties. Although he was one of the most outstanding boys at school, he had never given a party at his home. It was an occasion for him. There was something happy and almost innocent in his face that made me continue to look at him.

"Come on in, Ann," he said enthusiastically. "I thought maybe you weren't coming. It's getting sort of late."

I mumbled something and let him take my arm. The entrance of the house was formal and forbidding. In the hallway there was a statue of a cherub holding a pitcher, from which water poured into a shallow gray stone bowl. The rest of the house was just as forbidding: velvet-covered chairs, walls lined with books, and aristocratic heads perched on end tables.

"Pretty ritzy," I mumbled. I had known Jonathan only in the familiar context of Wilson, and wished suddenly I were anyplace but here.

"Oh, you know. Mother." Jonathan shrugged, then grinned. "Wait until you see the rec room."

The basement, which once must have been the typical old dark basement of the rich, had been turned into a giant rec room. All of it was paneled in very dark, beautiful wood. Yellow coach lamps were spaced on the wall to provide light; the floor was carpeted in deep red. At one end of the room was a large pool table; at the other end, where most of the party was, a magnificent fireplace of old brick. There was a player piano, which was playing now "Down by the Old Mill Stream." Jay Collins was pumping the pedals, and Jerry Adams and Guy Richards, who sometimes sang barbershop at assemblies, were harmonizing.

"Everyone seems to be here," I said, and grinned at Jonathan. I wondered how I could ever have been angry at him.

I have tried to remember, but cannot, if there was anything in those first hours of the party that was different from any other party. It was a happy, boisterous affair filled with lots of food and drink and the exuberance of spirits released for the summer. Behind the sound of kidding and joking was the background music of the player piano thumping out antiquated tunes. It was a party that verged hilariously on happy chaos, but never quite spilled over.

Then, at some undefined point, the character of the evening changed, like a car that has been running smoothly veering abruptly out of control and plunging over a dark precipice. Maybe it was the punch, but more likely it was an accumulation of grievances that had been stored up through the year: prizes and trophies lost, snubs, wrongs. In the center of it all stood Jonathan, tall and smiling and triumphant, the creator of Atlantis, member of the school board, winner of the trophy for The Most Outstanding Boy of the Year. His modesty and innocent happiness, here in this setting of wealth, must have been galling to the losers: those like Akins and Coster, who also ran, and Langley, who had cheated on a test.

Innocent insults became subtly something deeper.

"Hey, Jonathan, where you going to school?"

"He's going to Harvard—or Yale!" someone shouted.

"We are poor little lambs who have gone astray. Ba-ba-ba . . . " Akins sang.

Everyone laughed. Jonathan looked uncertain, then laughed, too, accepting it as a joke.

"He isn't going anywhere. They won't let him in!" Coster shouted.

More laughter.

"He's going to bum around the world. He's going to be a

hippie!" Coster cried, doubling over in a sudden convulsion of laughter.

"He's going to Mexico to sleep with the senoritas!" Langley yelled.

It was strange that Jonathan, who was usually so acute, didn't sense the faint scorn in the voices. Perhaps it was that he really was innocent, more innocent than the rest of us in some respect, or perhaps the success of the party had lulled him into some feeling of safety. I felt my heart began to hammer nervously.

"Let's dance," I said, looking around wildly for help. "Let's play some music and dance."

"Dance with a dolly with a hole in her stocking," a voice sang.

It was suddenly a very rowdy party, not a well-ordered one at all, but a brawl. "Come on, dance. Everybody dance!" someone shouted. A record player switched on.

I walked over to Jonathan. "Shall we go first?" I said.

"Sure—I—sure, okay."

We were the only ones on the floor. The others simply stood watching us. "End the party, Jonathan," I whispered. "They're getting drunk."

"It wasn't spiked that much," Jonathan said. "Don't worry."

The music ended. Still nobody volunteered to dance. Jonathan, trying to save the party, held out his arms.

"Next?" he said gaily. "Raymond? Okay." He grabbed Raymond Summers and whirled him around the floor a couple times. "We're in love," he said gaily.

Everyone laughed. The sound filled the room. It was an ugly laugh. Or perhaps that was only in my mind. Perhaps it was an innocent laugh, filled with gentle amusement at the sight of two boys dancing together, but I thought it was an ugly laugh. I stared at the two whirling boys, something exploding inside of my brain. Something sick wound through my stomach.

"Stop it!" I choked, and tore the two boys apart.

"Not stopping. Going to dance with Raymond all night," Jonathan mumbled stubbornly.

"For Pete's sakes—"

"Going to dance—all night—with Raymond—"

Some truth that hadn't quite been apparent seemed to dawn on the group. It was as if, by my actions, some dark connection had been made. The room was suddenly, abruptly filled with silence and shame, as if everyone regretted the scene.

"Okay—won't dance," Jonathan mumbled, drunk now. "Then better close up the old shop and all go home. Close up the old punch bowl, turn out the lights—"

"Yeah, it's getting late," Coster mumbled. His face was shocked, but then, even if he had been student-body president, he was only eighteen, too. He had seen very few kings fall.

Jonathan looked at us bleakly; then he suddenly became bitter. His chest heaved. "I don't care! See. I don't give a damn!" he said fiercely.

In that terrible moment I sickly realized two things: I had betrayed him, and he was innocent. My mind had made some erroneous connection.

At that moment the party ended, and people started going home.

"Great party, Jonathan," Coster mumbled.

"Gotta be going," Akins said heartily.

My last impression as I left the room was of that solitary figure standing at the door: Jonathan, who even in defeat seemed strangly unique. The anger had gone from his face now. He stood at the door as each person passed and courteously, almost gently, said his name and wished him goodnight. When it came my turn he spoke to me too, although our eyes didn't quite meet.

"Good night, friend."

I remember that very distinctly. He said it gravely, with respect and love.

The following night he tried to kill himself.

We had ridden our bicycles out to the Soldug River and sat looking out over the cool water.

"I'm sorry last night was such a disaster," Jonathan said. He sat hunched over, staring out at the river.

"It was all right," I protested. "Everyone had a good time."

"I guess Atlantis was just a dream." He spoke softly, his voice filled with emotion. "Nobody but me ever believed it."

I didn't answer. I didn't know what to say except that I loved him and that I knew he was innocent. But it was too late for that. Atlantis was gone and we both knew it.

My mouth opened to protest, but no sound came out. Pain stung my throat. It was the first time it had occurred to me, I think, that Jonathan was a vulnerable human being like any other boy and that he could be hurt. I darted a quick look at his face, then stared at the river, too miserable to speak.

Blindly my mind groped down through the murk of emotion, trying to find something in that abysmal darkness that would make me feel innocent. I didn't see how it could have happened, how I could have made that erroneous dark connection.

Oh, I knew. I knew, all right. Somehow my desire to have him tell me that he loved me had betrayed me. *Why* didn't he say he loved me? Not normal . . . Raymond Summers . . .

The only trouble was, it wasn't true at all. He was perfectly normal. As he had stood there at the party looking at all of us, that strange savage look on his face, I had known that he was just as normal as Coster or Akins or any other boy.

Jonathan rose and walked over to the empty rope that we used to swing out over the river. His fingers grasped the rope, and he swung out, then back.

"Hey," I said, alarmed, "you can't swim, remember?"

Jonathan, ready to swing out again, paused, half turning. There was a queer expression on his face. It was as if he were debating about me, then deciding that I had betrayed him, too. In that moment he relinquished my friendship. In a smoothly fluid, athletic motion, he raised himself to his toe tips and, grasping the rope firmly, swung out again.

It was like a motion he had rehearsed in his mind, a perfect basketball shot from midcourt. His body reached the end of the swing, arched, and in a perfect motion, dived straight downward.

It must have been a very deep, clean dive, one that took him to the bottom of the river. He must have hit his head on one of the large rocks that lay there, and the force of the blow must have knocked him unconscious for a moment, because he didn't come up. The ring swung back, and the river's surface became smooth again.

I stared at the water, so cool and dark and deep. He was gone. Then, with complete presence of mind, I dived in and started swimming.

I thrashed around and around in the water for perhaps five seconds before I found him. Then my fingers grasped his hair and pulled him to the surface. His mouth opened and closed like a fish, gasping for air; then a strangled, choking sound came from his throat. I saw his face, shocked and frightened. He looked at me wildly and began to thrash his arms in the water.

"Hang on to me. Don't fight!" I yelled desperately as he dragged me down.

Panic rose in his face. He flailed his arms and swung at me.

"What are you trying to do? Kill us both?" I yelled savagely.

Then darkness slowly descended upon me. I felt a throbbing pain in my head, and my body, swept away by the current, bumped into rocks and went down into blackness.

Eight

I woke up in a hospital. A nurse stood over me.

"Awake?" she said, and smiled.

I stared at her.

"Where am I?"

"You're in a hospital. You took quite a spill there in the river."

The river. Jonathan. I remembered now. He had swung out on the rope and dived into the river. I had gone after him. We had been struggling; he had swung at me with his arms and then—But my mind wouldn't go any further.

"What happened?" I said cautiously.

"Don't you know?"

"I can't remember," I said vaguely. At the edge of memory there was something dark and ugly that I wanted to forget.

"You hit your head on something. Probably rocks as you

were carried downstream. You were pretty bruised up. It's lucky your friend knew how to apply artificial respiration. That probably saved your life."

How had Jonathan got out? What had he done? Dragged me out of the river? On that opposite bank where the water ran swift and shallow, had he grabbed a log, managed somehow to regain his footing? But then, I remembered too, he had practically drowned me. I remembered that part very clearly. Maybe he had saved my life, but he had practically drowned me first.

I moved one leg and arm experimentally. The other arm hung limp. The other leg wouldn't move.

"My leg won't move," I said with surprise.

"Dr. Anderson will be in pretty soon. He'll explain everything," the nurse said. As she left, Dr. Anderson, our family doctor, came through the doorway.

"Well," he said, "we're awake. How are we feeling, Ann?"

"My leg—"

Dr. Anderson cleared his throat. "You have a blood clot on the brain stem. That is why you can't move your arm or leg. We have medicines to dissolve clots. You'll just have to lie quiet for a few weeks and let it dissolve."

I swallowed. "What if it doesn't—dissolve?"

"There's always the possibility of further damage."

Further damage? What did he mean, further damage?

"Medicine isn't perfectly predictable. But for now you'll just rest and lie still for a few weeks. We're moving you to a nursing home this afternoon."

I continued to look at him.

"The emergency is over. It's just a question of time and nature. You'll stay there until you can go home. Okay?"

I didn't answer. I didn't want to go to a nursing home. I didn't want to have an arm and leg that wouldn't move. I didn't want a blood clot on the brain stem. *Brain stem.*

Jonathan appeared an hour later, looking strangely formal in slacks and a brown sport jacket, and holding a sheath of florist's flowers in one hand. At Wilson, an air of ease and grace had always accompanied Jonathan's movements. Now he looked awkward and humble, so strange that I stared at him. Standing there, he reminded me peculiarly of the pictures you see of foreign immigrants.

"Hello, friend. I brought you a present." He tried to smile, a stiff, unnatural smile that slid over his face and disappeared in misery.

I stared at him. I couldn't believe it. Flowers. "Thanks," I said tonelessly.

"I thought—" He looked helplessly for some place to get rid of the flowers and finally found the nightstand.

Hate surged through me. He had practically killed us both, and now he was smiling his fake smile, holding out flowers. The fact that he had probably saved my life held no weight at the moment. All I could see was that healthy body and fake smile.

"As long as you've brought them, leave them."

"Look, Ann, I don't blame you for being mad," Jonathan said uneasily.

"I'm not mad."

"I know I practically drowned you. I panicked when I realized I couldn't swim," he said simply. I stared at him until he looked out the window. "I hope you can forgive me for that."

"I forgive you. Of course I forgive you," I said impatiently.

The lie slid out so easily that it sounded like truth. Surprisingly, Jonathan accepted the words as truth. But then he wanted to believe them, I thought. He probably felt guilty. Why shouldn't he? Inside, some cold part of me remained like stone, unforgiving. I hated him. I hated him for looking miserable. I hated him for being such an oddball. Because of him, I wasn't going to college. Because of him, I had a blood clot. On the brain stem. One tiny change of position— And he stood there smiling. I couldn't forgive him for that. I would never forgive him for that.

Jonathan made a sort of jerky movement that brought him closer to the bed. "They tell me you're going to be all right."

"There's a blood clot. *If* it dissolves I'll be all right," I corrected.

"It'll dissolve."

Since he wasn't a medical student, his diagnosis seemed a little out of place. "I can't lift my arm. One leg won't move at all."

"Look—it could be worse, couldn't it?" Jonathan's hand made a desperate motion.

Naturally he didn't want it bad since he had caused it, I thought. Naturally he wanted it to be something simple like a headache, where you took a couple of aspirins and cured it.

"This afternoon they're moving me to a nursing home. I may be there for months. People die in nursing homes," I said coldly. One part of my mind felt pity for him; another childish part wanted to see him on his knees weeping with remorse and grief.

"You're not going to die," Jonathan said impatiently. "And I'll come see you every day. I promise."

"I don't want you to. You'd hate it. I don't want you there."

Jonathan stared at me, then walked to the window. "I know you don't mean what you're saying now, Ann," he said. "You're a little woozy with all that medicine. I'll come."

A few minutes later, when he left, he repeated the promise. "Don't worry. I'll be there," he said, and I heard his footsteps go *clip, clip* down the hall. The taps had been there all year. He had never obeyed Herrider's order to take them off.

After Jonathan left, a nurse came in. "Well, we're looking better today."

I hated her, too; I hated all nurses with their fake, cheerful voices.

"Shall we get some clothes on? It's moving day."

I noticed that nurses and doctors used the pronoun *we* improperly. *We* will have to eat and get well. *We* are looking better today. The odd mannerism was distracting. Obviously they did not mean *we* at all, but *you*.

The nurse was helping me into clothes, sliding them over my head. "Your parents will be here in a few minutes," she said finally when I didn't move to help.

A half hour later I was lifted carefully into a car and transported across town to the nursing home, Quiet Oaks, named that, no doubt, because three oak trees stood in front of it. The building was a long, low, one-story affair with lots of glass and sunlight.

I watched helplessly as two girls came out and lifted me into a wheelchair. Frantically I signaled to my parents not to let them take me inside; then we were going through a doorway.

Old people, strapped in wheelchairs, swarmed around the main lobby and nurse's station. There was an odd odor that I couldn't place. I felt as if I were going to be sick. *Further damage.* What did that mean, further damage?

A pretty woman named Mrs. McClellan came forward and introduced herself.

"You must be Ann," she said, and smiled at me. She had the same cheerful voice as the nurses at the hospital. "Your room is number fourteen. We're rather crowded now, so it's the only room available."

I stared at a man who was approaching us in a wheelchair. He had a grotesque, frozen grin on his face and was propelling himself in a kind of lurching motion toward us. For me, only young people existed in the world. And young people, even the homeliest, are somewhat attractive. I had never thought of old people at all, except to know in a cursory way that they existed someplace. I found the deformity ugly and shocking. I smiled feebly, so no one could see my feelings.

"If you like, we'll go right down and get settled in; then I'll talk to your parents," Mrs. McClellan said.

Two girls in white uniforms came up and wheeled me down the hallway. Closing a curtain in the room, they undressed me and lifted me into a narrow bed with very clean white sheets. One of them stooped and cranked up the bed so I was half sitting up. Then they pulled back the curtain, and my parents came in.

"Well, it looks like a nice place," my father said awkwardly.

"Yes, it does, doesn't it?" Mother said, her voice rising hopefully. Her glance skidded nervously around the room, taking in two other beds and their occupants, the walls, and a piece of equipment on a nightstand that looked official and deadly; I found out later it was a suction machine. "I don't think it'll be half bad," Mother said, her voice sounding fake and cheerful like an echo of the nurses.

"Well, I suppose we should be going," my father said.

"You're not leaving yet, are you?" I said in an alarmed voice, and they stayed awhile longer.

In the bed next to me an old woman with wild white hair sat up and said loudly and emphatically, "My name is Jule Richards."

"Hello, Jule." My mother, trying to be friendly, smiled.

"My name is Jule Richards!"

Mother and Father exchanged startled looks, then looked at me covertly.

"Her name is Jule Richards," I said bleakly. The woman repeated again, enunciating clearly and distinctly, "My name is Jule Richards," the only words she ever said, I found out later.

"You can't expect—" Mother began. Her glance wavered hopefully to the third bed. It held a middle-aged woman, thin as a dry stick, who looked back at us and said nothing at all.

An uneasy feeling began to form inside me, a really odd feeling that started in my mind and worked its way down the length of my body. I frantically tried to move my leg, but it wouldn't budge. Neither would my arm. It was hopeless. A strange odor clung to my nostrils; there was an odd metallic taste in my mouth. I felt as if I needed to brush my teeth.

The sun's last rays were fanning out under a rim of clouds in the west, and already the room held the feel of evening coming, a certain duskiness. Some quietness had come into the building.

"Don't go yet," I said in a hoarse voice, grabbing Mother's hand.

"We'll come back tomorrow," she said.

"Don't make it hard for your mother," Father said sternly.

"It won't be for long." And reluctantly I let go of her hand.

A bell rang deep in the recesses of the building. A girl came with a dinner tray. She placed it on a stand, took a spoonful of mashed potatoes, and lifted it to my mouth.

"I can feed myself."

"Oh, can you? Good." She handed me the spoon.

"I'm not hungry," I mumbled as she stood watching.

"All right," she said cheerfully. "I'll leave your tray here. You might like it later."

When she was gone, I awkwardly aimed a spoon of mashed potatoes toward my mouth. It missed my mouth and hit my nose. Mashed potatoes slid down the side of my face and landed in a whitish clump in my gown. I tried another bite, and the spoon tipped over, one side of it clinking against my teeth.

In the bed by the window the woman who had said nothing up to this point said in a matter-of-fact voice, "You better tell them you can't feed yourself."

I looked out the window and didn't answer. I didn't feel like talking. I hated the place. I tried cautiously to lift my leg again, straining until my hands were covered with perspiration. Then I remembered the blood clot and stopped, lying very still. I had the fear that if I jarred the blood clot, it would move. And then I would die, I thought, my throat suddenly dry with fear. Let it dissolve, I prayed. Let it go away.

And tomorrow Jonathan would come. He had promised.

Down the hall a man started calling out rhetorically, "I don't want to die. Tell me how not to die; tell me how not to die." I looked at my roommate, startled.

"That's Jacobs. They ought to knock him out," she said indignantly. "They would in a hospital."

With darkness, the building grew quiet, and the old people started shuffling down the hall toward bed, the ambulatory hanging on to the side rails, those in wheelchairs softly wheeling down the carpeted corridors. Girls came in, expertly flipped over the woman called Jule, and changed her bed. "My name is Jule Richards!" she shouted aggressively.

The woman next to the window was given a sponge bath. The faint pleasant smell of powder and soap rose in the air. She looked even thinner naked. The bones of her chest protruded, and she had shrunk to the size of a child. *Cancer.*

The barrel of dirty linen rolled out the door, and the light switched off abruptly, so that the only light visible was one in the hallway. I listened to the barrel as it rattled down the hall and to the sound of the girls talking; then they were gone, and the room was quiet except for the sound of breathing.

I felt resistance building in my chest.

A nurse came in. She carried a long needle, and now she began to fill it. "No!" I said in a horrified voice, and kicked at her fiercely.

Two other girls came in to help. One of them held down my leg. A feeling of hate surged through me, black and ugly. My good arm flailed out. I was breathing very fast, I saw their mouths: surprised, then sober and determined. Then the needle stung my thigh.

In the middle of the night someone came into the room and switched on the light. I blinked and looked at a huge woman in a nightgown who was standing by the foot of my bed. She moved about the room picking afghans off the other two beds and stacking them in a pile on the foot of my bed. Now she began to take the pictures off the walls and piled them on top of the afghans.

"Get out," I hissed, staring at her in horror. She ignored me and continued busily gathering articles and arranging them on my bed. "They're gifts," she explained.

"Get out," I whispered, fumbling for a bell at the end of a cord, finally finding it.

Steps came swiftly down the hall, and two girls came into the room. "It's the new one," one of the girls said despairingly. "What's her name?"

"Lytle."

"Come on, Mrs. Lytle," the girl said. Her voice was coaxing, rather cajoling. "Your room is down here, Mrs. Lytle."

The old woman looked at them suspiciously. Something cunning and stubborn came into her face. From the darkness in her mind, there arose a reservoir of resistance. One of the girls took her arm gently and, with surprising strength for an old woman, she broke away.

"These are mine," she said fiercely, hanging on to the afghans.

Another girl came in to help. There were three of them now, struggling with the old woman. One of them got behind and pushed, and the other two tried to drag her out of the room.

I had been frightened at first, and on the side of the girls. Now abruptly my feelings swung in the opposite direction, and I felt a surge of identity with the old woman as her elbows and feet lashed out and hit at her captors. She was like a calf that has been led meekly to the slaughterhouse, where, with some realization of its destination coming to it, it turns and fights back with abnormal strength.

Her violence shocked the girls, and they loosened their grip.

"I'm going home!" I felt a flick of triumph as the old woman burst out of their grasp and strode toward the door, afghans clutched in her arms.

They finally subdued her. Four of them and a needle finally overpowered her, and she went along meekly to her room. Afterward I lay staring at the wall. People were not as simple as I supposed and not so accepting of their fate as others liked to think.

My heart was beating very fast. I couldn't go to sleep again for a long time. My mind skidded from spot to spot: Wilson, Atlantis, Jonathan, the old woman and her fierce resistance.

When my mother came the following morning, I completely went to pieces. I grabbed her hand. "Please—please get me out of here," I begged.

Nine

The philosophy of the nursing home was quite simple. They simply accepted the death of everyone who entered their doors. All activity, all routine, was programmed for making death as pleasant and unobtrusive as possible.

Jonathan's philosophy was just the opposite. He ignored death completely. It simply didn't exist.

I described the routine to him two days later. The strangeness of the place must have made an impression on my mind, because I discovered I was whispering. "Everyone has to go to 'Activities.' It's a rule. You can't get out of them. And you have to get up at six in the morning. They wash your face with a cold cloth."

Jonathan gave me a long measuring look. "I wish you would get it out of your head that this is a nursing home," he said. "You're not in a nursing home."

I stared at him, thinking for a moment that he had lost his mind.

"There aren't any nursing homes in Atlantis," Jonathan said.

"Better watch that sort of talk around her. They'll strap you on a stretcher and send you to the funny farm."

"In Atlantis one rules oneself. One isn't *forced* to play games or *forced* to smile."

"Here comes a nurse," I said warningly.

"I don't see any nurses," Jonathan said. "No, you're mistaken. That's a waitress." He smiled at the nurse coming in the door with a tray. "Oh, room service," he said. "We'll have two bottles of Coke, miss."

The girl in white smiled back at him. "Certainly, sir."

"See," Jonathan said. "Just room service."

I smiled feebly.

Nurses and doctors did not exist for him. People did not die in the night; they were called home on urgent business. I did not believe Jonathan, of course. I wasn't so crazy that I completely closed my eyes to reality, but I went along with it because anything was better than being reduced to a name on a wrist bracelet, making pom-poms out of yarn, and singing songs about its being a great new day.

Jonathan improvised a game with various elaborations. The daily newspaper was the *Atlantis Bulletin*. The crossword puzzle in it was Casey's Quiz. To get a passing grade, you had to work it without a dictionary in a half hour. Fifteen minutes earned an A. Twenty minutes was a B. Anything over a half hour meant you had flunked, and Jonathan kept scrupulous tally in a black notebook.

The therapy he insisted on was calisthenics. Mimicking

111

Hopkin's voice in football drill, he made me raise my arm ten times. When I protested he savagely said, "You want to get well, don't you? You want to get out of here, don't you?"

"Of course I want—"

"Well then, get that arm in shape!"

One day Jonathan unceremoniously dumped a load of library books on the stand.

"You've had a long-enough vacation. It's time you went to work."

I picked up one of the books and looked at the title. *College Composition.* "What are these for?" I said shakily.

"I'm priming you for the U in January. I'm your tutor."

"You're crazy! I'll never get out of here."

"January, friend. Here are your assignments for the week. You've already lost half a year."

"I'm not sure I even want to go," I protested.

"Of course you're going. We're both going. I've already sent in my application—so you better make it." He pointed out my assignment. "I'll be back tomorrow to see how you've done."

After he left I stared at the walls. College. In January.

"My name is Jule Richards!" Jule said emphatically.

The cancer patient watched me silently.

"He's crazy," I said angrily. "He's off his rocker. I'll be dead by January!"

"You aren't going to die," she said in the matter-of-fact voice she always used. "They put the ones who are really sick at the other end of the hall."

A week later *she* was moved to the other end of the hall. I felt sad, and then unaccountably relieved, as I remembered her words. I was too selfish to be concerned long about

112

someone else's misfortune. From the safety of the West Wing I watched Jonathan come striding up the walk.

"Today we're going to take ten laps around the building in your wheelchair," he said cheerfully.

He grabbed the handlebars of the wheelchair and maneuvered me out the door. I hadn't been out of my room much, and some of the patients stared at me. I stared back, shocked more than I cared to admit by their disabilities.

"That's Harry Edwards," I said. "One of the patients. He's got some horrible disease. I don't know what it is, but they say—"

"I don't see any patients," Jonathan said, looking around, a blank look on his face.

"I guess you're right," I said lamely. "It's just Herrider."

The thought amused Jonathan. "I noticed that, too. He does look like Herrider, doesn't he?"

We both laughed, remembering the tyrannical reign of Herrider at Wilson. And suddenly other patients looked like people we'd known all our lives. We made it a game, matching them with familiar names. When Jonathan left, gratitude swept over me. I hadn't forgiven him. We had never mentioned the fact that he had tried to kill himself. He had saved me. Tears sprang into my eyes. In contrast to the nursing home, Jonathan was everything that was whole and good. The one shining thing in the world. To him I was still an individual—not just human, but a special human being who lived in Atlantis and still strived for some high place.

The quality of those days was marked by soaring hope that often plummeted to black despair. The climate of that whole October was uneven, with pouring rain battering the landscape one day and a wild wind tearing the clouds into shreds the next. One night a full harvest moon hung in the sky, with a cloud like a charred limb over its face.

It was on the night of the full moon that superstition overrode reason, and the patients turned restless. I could hear their voices rising in a troubled chorus, and then abruptly a strange, wild, incredible scene erupted. The fire alarm went off—*bong-bong-bong*—fire doors slammed, the siren wailed, and the fire department arrived.

Often on nights when there was a moon someone would wander away. The warning bell on the back door would buzz frantically, and then there would be the sight of flashlights in the dark as a frantic search was conducted in all the rooms for the missing patient.

Jacobs, tranquilized into submissiveness usually, would yell in a weird staccato monotone, "I'm crazy. I'm not crazy. They're going to put a stick in my mouth. Crazy. Not crazy."

"Shut up!"

"Stick. Stick in my mouth."

"We are all going to hell!" another patient, Louise Manner, would shout ominously. "We are all going to hell!"

"Stop praying!" Jacobs would call fiercely. "I don't want anyone praying for me! I *want* to go to hell!"

And then another voice would rise sweetly and join the chorus. "Operator. Op-er-a-tor—"

My roommate would rise up, startled, in bed. "My name is Jule Richards," she would cry.

Like lost souls floating outward from earth in some limbo of fog and darkness, their voices called out to each other in the night.

Out in the darkness the flashlights searched the frozen fields, swept over stiff weeds, rooftops and fences. Then, in relief, they would spot the shivering escapee huddled in a field, and he would be brought back to safety and warmth, fed warm liquid, and put back into bed. And the night would end finally, fatigue eventually winding down the voices.

On nights when the moon was full, patients mysteriously died. The aides in the nursing home superstitiously believed they died in "threes." "They always go in threes," they would whisper to each other, and they would wait, after the first, for the second and then the third.

But I do not believe it is true that people die in threes. People always die one by one.

October was an uneven month and I vacillated like the weather, from hope of college in January, to sure despair.

"Six steps," Jonathan said triumphantly one day. "Tomorrow we'll do ten."

"I can't make it," I gasped, sinking back into the wheelchair. My leg was trembling. My hands were clammy with perspiration.

"Ten tomorrow," Jonathan said crisply.

"What are we practicing for—the Olympics?" I said bitterly.

Jonathan, stung, looked at me. He shrugged. "Okay—okay if you don't want to try."

"I am trying," I protested.

"You're not trying. You're holding back. You're afraid of hurting yourself," Jonathan said matter-of-factly.

I didn't answer. Dr. Anderson had assured me it was all right to walk, but I couldn't rid myself of the fear that the blood clot was still there, undissolved, and that if it moved, I would die.

"I don't want to go to college," I said sullenly.

115

"Okay—forget it."

"I'm tired of playing games."

There was a long, uninterrupted silence when neither of us spoke. I realized that to Jonathan, of course, it hadn't been a game, just as Atlantis hadn't been a game. He actually believed I would walk, go to college in January; it was like the dream of Atlantis that he had made a whole class somehow believe in for a year. I would walk again and be as good as new.

"I didn't know you felt that way. I didn't know you felt it was just a game. I thought you wanted to go to college."

"Well, I don't," I said.

"You just want to sit in a wheelchair all your life."

"That's right."

Jonathan laughed. "You kill me, Ann."

I stared at him belligerently.

"You had me fooled for a minute," Jonathan said. "I thought you were serious. Okay. Eight tomorrow. We'll take it slow and easy."

He won me over with his persistence. Gradually I fell into the spell of his logic: there was no nursing home; there were no patients; it was all just an extension of Wilson and Atlantis.

The old people were still there, of course, and the strange, restrictive routine, but more and more it faded and just Jonathan and I were left, preparing for the U in January with books, exercises, and the taking of just one more fumbling step on the handbars.

The nurses did not go along with it entirely. They had seen too many relapses and were geared to anticipate the worst, but they relaxed the rules somewhat. Even they, I think, were caught up in the spell of Jonathan's hope and persuasion. Temporarily they allowed me to belong to the world of the living. Dr. Anderson brought me a college algebra book from home. One of the nurses made a mobile with U written across it, and it swung from a string over my bed.

The last weekend of October I went home for two days. It was a gray, cloudy, dismal world outside the window, but for me the sun shone brightly. I wheeled around the house and laughed for no reason; I fed the goldfish, helped bake cookies, and stayed up until one o'clock at night watching TV. I raided the refrigerater and drank Coke and slept until ten o'clock in the morning. Then I got up and phoned everybody I knew who was still in town.

I had lost track of school gossip; now, as if I had never been gone, I heard all the familiar names. Akins and Coster were at the U; the Mercer twins had both joined the Navy. Jimmy Walker had broken up with Carol Marshall when he came home on leave, and had eloped with Alice Winters, a junior cheerleader. Carol Marshall came over in the evening and confirmed this news.

"I'm sorry," I said. I felt awkward and didn't know what to say. We sat in the rec room, the record player emitting a sad song, and I felt her unhappiness fill the room.

"It was just one of those things," Carol said, her voice like breaking glass. "He was writing to Alice, I guess, too, all the time. When he came home, they saw each other, and it just happened. Just like that."

"What are you going to do?" I asked.

"I don't know. I don't want to stay in town. I have an aunt in California. I might go down there." She twisted her hands uncertainly. "What about Jonathan and you?"

"We're still friends. Just good friends," I said. "We're both

117

going to the U in January." It was the first time I had actually said the words out loud, or admitted that they were a possibility.

"Jonathan was always someone special for you, wasn't he?"

I didn't answer. How could you explain someone like Jonathan or what he meant? Jonathan and I had never defined the relationship. We had never said the things lovers say; we had never kissed and lied and quarreled, and kissed and lied again.

What did it mean, love? I lay in bed and thought about it that night. Loving someone. Being in love. Was it the way it was with Carol, a terrible pain of loss? Was it the girls at the nursing home lifting broken bodies carefully, softly laughing with a senile patient? Or was it Jonathan's hand gently closing over mine, Jonathan grimly prodding me to walk, to get that mind in shape—for God's sakes, get that mind in shape!

Monday morning, back at the nursing home again, I looked at Jonathan's face closely. I couldn't tell what he was thinking. What would he do if I suddenly, today, told him I loved him? But that was crazy, too. How could you seriously love an oddball like Jonathan? And his looks—he seemed like a demented scarecrow.

He was Jonathan the Coach today, brisk, businesslike, as he wheeled me out into the hallway to walk.

"We'll try twenty steps today," he said cheerfully, helping me out of the wheelchair.

"Twenty? Are you out of your mind?" I snarled. With every single step I was terrified; with every single step my mind protested. Yet every day I allowed him to prod me into one more.

I put my hand cautiously on the rail and swung to a standing position, his arm supporting my waist. My legs started to move. One—two—three. So far, so good.

"Ten—eleven—twelve," Jonathan counted triumphantly. "We'll try for twenty." Without missing count, he turned me around and headed me back down the hall. "Thirteen— fourteen—

"Fifteen—sixteen—" he counted like a drill seargent.

Our feet got tangled up as I took the next step. Somehow he lost his grip on me. I felt his arm shift on my waist and felt myself wavering. Then I lost my grip on the rail, lost my balance, pitched forward, and crashed to the floor.

A stricken look swept over Jonathan's face. Awkwardly, silently, he helped me up. A surge of anger shot through me.

"What are you trying to do? Kill me again?" I said stiffly.

The unbelievable words had come out of my mouth.

We stared at each other for one long, terrible moment. His face whitened as if I had slapped him. There was a shocked, stunned expression on his face. Then in a little, lurching, jerky motion, he turned and walked away.

After a long time I wheeled back to my room, my heart pounding. So it wasn't forgotten. It had been there all the time, lying under the fall days, a dark pebble under a rock.

I had never forgotten. I had never really forgiven.

Ten

N either Jonathan nor I ever mentioned those words
again, and neither of us ever forgot them. They lay
below the surface of the winter days, something too
shocking to be forgotten, too tremendous to speak about
casually, so that in the end we both pretended they weren't
there.

But, no matter how many steps I took, I knew that
Jonathan never forgot, as I never forgot, that once I had
fallen, that once I had said savagely, "What are you trying to
do? Kill me again?" He always made sure his grip was firm; I
always made sure I never fell again.

In some strange way the knowledge of that difference
between us that could never be talked about drew us closer
together. We were more careful of each other, kinder in
those days, but maybe that is only my imagination, maybe it

was only because Christmas was coming and everyone was suddenly kinder anyway, and I would be going home.

In a rush of holiday spirits, I relented and joined the activities of the other patients. Already seeing myself a visitor, hale and hearty and mobile, I sat in the Activities Room and cut out dozens of stars, made table decorations, strung popcorn. I made a wreath for the door of my room, and then, in a burst of generosity, made two other Christmas decorations for the doors of two patients who were bedfast and had no relatives.

As once I had refused to join the activities, seeing them as an insult to the intelligence of any human being, I now played bingo with buttons and wheelchair basketball, and listened to groups singing Christmas carols. Evenings when she had no one else to play with, I played gin rummy with an old lady named Maud, who had been a schoolteacher in Montana. She forgot her cards and cheated, and I let her, suddenly benevolent and charitable, because I was going home.

"Well, well, we're getting along fine," Dr. Anderson said jovially as he made his rounds the week before Christmas.

"Can I go home this week?" I begged.

"Go home this week," he repeated, debating.

"Oh, please. I'm feeling fine."

"You're not completely out of the woods, you know, Ann."

"Yes, I am. I can walk three times around the building— and if I'm going to college in January I have to stop acting like an invalid pretty soon."

"Maybe you ought to wait a year."

"A year!"

Dr. Anderson smiled at the look on my face. "I can't

believe you've progressed so well, I guess. It's just the cautious doctor in me. All right. You may go home. But only for four days. I want a complete checkup before you leave for school. And I want to take some X rays, so the day after Christmas back you come. Promise?"

"If I can go home now—yes, I promise."

He left and I started packing. Jonathan came in. "Where do you think you're going?" he said, looking at the suitcase, his eyebrows lifting.

"Home," I said blithely.

"Really? For good?" he said cautiously.

"Till the day after Christmas. It's the same as going home for good. I only have to come back for a checkup and X rays."

"I'll drive you."

"We'll have to check with the nurses' station."

"Naturally we have to check with them," Jonathan said with heavy sarcasm, and he gave a sigh of despair, his eyebrows lifting in the direction of the office.

"It's not so bad a place." I could afford to be generous; I was leaving.

Jonathan snorted. "If it hadn't been for me you'd still be in bed. They'd had you dead and buried."

It was true. Without him, I would have been just another patient; I never would have made it. But then if it hadn't been for him I wouldn't have been here in the first place, a point I did not mention out loud. Besides, I was well. I was going home.

"Come on, let's get out of here," Jonathan said as I paused in the hallway. He was carrying my suitcase, impatiently shifting from one foot to the other.

Outside, I looked back. The building was pretty with

Christmas. A giant fir tree stood in the visitor's lounge, its lights blinking. Baskets of flowers and poinsettias stood on the counter. Organizations had donated decorations, and the lobby looked like the elaborate, fashionable entrance of a grand hotel.

"What are you doing?" Jonathan said.

"Just looking at the lights."

"Hey, you're not getting homesick for that place, are you?" he said, disgusted.

"No."

"You're out. You're free." He did a soldier's march on the sidewalk, singing in his off-key tenor, "You're out of the ar-my, Mister Jones—"

I think I realized in that moment how much Jonathan had hated the place, perhaps more than I. He had hated its regimentation and evil smells, its cloying whisper of death and decay. I don't think he really hated the personnel; it was death he hated because he loved life so much. Now as he drove along the street he began to talk about college, his voice eager and excited.

"I suppose the competition will be tough. There'll be a lot of sharp guys there," he said in a measuring voice, but he sounded sharp, too, ready to go.

I had taken his presence and time for granted; now I realized what a sacrifice it actually had been. Already a year older than the rest of us, Jonathan must have ached to go on to school, throw his good mind into the challenge of other minds. Instead, he had waited for me. Every day faithfully he had been there with his courage and unshakable belief.

"I suppose all the clothes styles have changed," I said, thinking that I, too, felt ready to go on.

Jonathan grinned and lifted his eyebrows. To him clothes presented no problem; in college he would be as out of style as he had been in high school. Yet somehow he would fit, I realized. He would mesmerize a class with an idea like Atlantis, or an idea of something else. It was his nature to lead; it was as natural to him as oil rising to the top of water.

At home the house was decorated for the holidays: fir boughs on the mantel, blue and white satin balls, a tree loaded with silver tinsel, and familiar ornaments. Downtown, stores were filled with clothes for the holidays, fake snow, Santa Clauses. Bells and candy canes, already bedraggled and shabby from rain, hung on street lamps. Over the town, projected from a loudspeaker system, there floated the solemn and joyous sound of Christmas music.

In the falling dusk, as I walked beside Jonathan and listened to the music, I felt lifted out of myself. Jonathan stopped talking. His face became sober and thoughtful, and then his hand reached down to fold over my hand. Later in the car he drove with one hand, his other hand on top of mine. Once our glances met, and we both grinned in a sappy way.

At home, Mother said, "You'll stay for dinner, won't you?"

"If it isn't any trouble," Jonathan said, answering as if his mind were someplace else. Ordinarily he would have refused.

I turned on the tree lights, and we sat looking at them, holding hands. Then finally the spell was broken; Mother called us to dinner.

My father engaged Jonathan in a conversation about college. Did he have any idea what he wanted to be? Did he

124

think liberal arts offered as much of a future as it used to? Or was the next era to be an age of technicians and scientists? "Maybe we are moving in that direction," my father said, "where technology rules society and meets so much of its demands that the liberal arts are no longer relevant."

"Men's ideas always will be relevant," Jonathan said. "Don't you think? I mean—there has to be someone to interpret the people," he said with his winning smile. It was Jonathan at his most persuasive: respectful, polite, almost apologetic about pointing out some particular point, a mannerism that even adults found beguiling since most adolescents make their point by arguing belligerently.

"But just as a practical matter of getting a job—"

"I guess I don't care to be practical, sir," Jonathan said.

"I think you're right, too," my father said, smiling his own charming smile back. "In theory. Frankly, I hope Ann specifically trains for a job. I think every girl should have some job she's trained to do."

After dinner Jonathan and I played cribbage. I played a haphazard game as always, not caring really whether I won or not. Jonathan played, as he did everything else, with fierce competitiveness. It never occurred to him in a game to let a weaker opponent win. To him that was as much cheating as throwing a game. Consequently, after a while, I felt myself playing fiercely too.

But in the middle of the game I suddenly felt tired, exhausted.

"You all right?" Jonathan looked at me sharply.

I nodded and continued to play, but a funny feeling of weakness spread through me. It suddenly felt like too much of an effort to pick up the tiny cribbage pegs and put them in place. One of the pegs slipped from my fingers and fell on the floor. I leaned down to retrieve it and couldn't lift my arm.

"I'll get it," Jonathan said.

"That's all right. I'll—" I forgot what I was going to say, couldn't remember. I stared at him and realized he was staring back.

My mouth must have formed words, but the sound of speech didn't come out. A garbled, blurred sound fell from my lips, then nothing. *I can't remember*, I thought, surprised.

A shocked look spread over Jonathan's face. I realized I had seen the look once before—the night Fuddy died.

"Don't try to move. Sit right there," he said, and he sprang out of the chair. It occurred to me that he was moving very fast.

A moment later I heard my father on the phone frantically calling Dr. Anderson. Soon I was being lifted into the car and then carried back to a bed, and Dr. Anderson's voice was saying to a nurse:

"It looks like another blood clot."

His face was blurred and far away yet his voice was very distinct, professionally brisk. His eyes looked through me and around me as if I had ceased to exist.

"Aphasia, I think. The loss of speech. And probably most motor coordination. We'll have to try using an alphabet board for some sort of communication," he said. "Maybe later—"

A bedrail snapped into place with a familiar click; a bell sounded somewhere in the building; I saw Jonathan's shocked face again.

And with the three things—the click of the bedrail, the bell, and Jonathan's face—the calm of the season was shattered. I knew that the happy life I had known had ended forever.

Eleven

Nothing in life had ever prepared Jonathan for defeat. Overlaying those halcyon days at Wilson, there had always been the continuing atmosphere of triumph, of victories sought and won with Jonathan in the center of it, always more warrior than student, modestly crowned with a laurel wreath.

It never occurred to him, I believe, that the other side of the coin of victory is defeat, that the counterpart of life is death, and that all purpose aimed at the highest has as a consequence the possibility of falling.

So now it did not occur to him, either, that a door had irrevocably clanged shut. He came into the room prepared for battle, prepared to play the game he had played before. There was no nursing home; there were no nurses or doctors. People did not die; they went home to take care of some urgent business. There had been a setback, but he had done it before; he could do it again.

Cheerful, smiling, he entered the room, armed with a load of Christmas presents and a board with the letters of the alphabet on it, his cheeks bright with December cold.

It was Christmas Eve. The general air of gloom and pessimism at Quiet Oaks had been replaced for the evening with an atmosphere of optimism, goodwill, and hilarity. In the lounge, a party was in progress; all ambulatory patients had gone down to it, and now through the hallways there came the sound of laughter and general confusion, and then the singular sound of a piano playing a Christmas song: "Come, all ye faithful, joyful and triumphant."

"Merry Christmas," Jonathan said, his voice booming out in the room like a cheerful cannon.

Up to this point I had not said a word. I had no inclination to say a word. In fact, it was impossible for me to say a word. I had tried secretly a couple of times to say "hello." It had come out something like "ho." After that I had kept my mouth firmly clamped shut.

I didn't answer, but made a futile gesture with my hand, which could have meant anything. Jonathan accepted it as a greeting and pulled up a chair by the bed.

Critically his brown eyes surveyed the damage. If he had been shocked, he didn't show it now by any change of expression on his face. It was obvious that since I didn't move, I couldn't. Someone had undoubtedly told him that I also couldn't speak.

"It looks like the U is out for January," he said in a matter-of-fact voice. "We'll aim at next fall."

I didn't answer, and he stood up and roamed around the

bed, his hands jammed in his pockets. "That's a better time anyway. We'll be entering with the rest of the class. Fall seventy-eight. We'll plan on that."

I wanted to speak then. I wanted to yell, "You're crazy. You're off your rocker. There isn't going to be any college in seventy-eight or any other time!" But I continued to stare at him, hypnotized by his cheerful voice and confidence.

"I've brought you a board," he said. "I've put all the letters of the alphabet on it. You can point to them and talk to me." He propped the piece of cardboard on the bed so I could reach it.

I hesitated. I had nothing to say to him or anyone else. I felt like a fool.

"Go ahead. Try it."

I jabbed my finger angrily at a letter. My finger, of course, missed the letter I was aiming at and knocked the board over. Jonathan replaced it without comment.

"Try again."

I got coordinated enough finally to spell out falteringly, MERRY CHRISTMAS.

"The same to you," Jonathan said triumphantly.

Thump-thump—I'm still alive—I'm in here. I'm a human being. *Thump—thump.*—Tears sprang to my eyes. The simple communication shook me up as much as if I'd been declared dead and my heart had suddenly, miraculously, started beating again.

I stared at the picture on the wall, then sullenly back at him. I didn't want him to see my emotion, to sense that incredible leap of hope in my heart. If he saw that, he would also sense the panic that had engulfed me when I realized I couldn't talk, might never be able to speak to anyone again.

130

"Try it a little slower this time." Jonathan grinned. "Aren't you anxious to see what present I brought you?"

"Y-E-S."

Despite myself, I was eager to see what was in the tiny box. He had never given me a real present before. I noted too that it was a different-shaped box than the one that had been on the car seat the other day, which meant he had bought it today. It also meant that the other present, something for college, probably, had suddenly been inappropriate; he had hurriedly substituted this present for it.

The tiny box contained a friendship ring, a gold band with a basket-weave pattern. It fit my third finger perfectly. Asked beforehand, I would have said it was a gift more suitable for one girl to give to another. Now that it was on my finger, I felt that it was exactly what I had always wanted. But then I think, too, that anything Jonathan gave me that day would have been exactly what I wanted.

We opened up the other presents. There was a mobile with Peanuts swinging from a string and an "Atlantis" school banner that he had stamped out of felt.

"I thought you could hang it on the wall," Jonathan said. "The walls are sort of grim-looking."

I thanked him, and we talked about Christmas for another half hour. It was growing dark outside.

"I have to go now," Jonathan said finally. Our hands clung together like magnets.

I nodded. His mother would be waiting. There would be his own Christmas tree, his own presents to open.

"We're going to Portland for a couple of days, but I'll be back next week."

I looked down at the ring and smiled. My finger spelled

out the words on the board, *thump—thump—*"I love it."

Jonathan smiled and left the room. I heard the *click-click* of his heels going down the hallway.

Later my parents came and opened up the rest of my gifts. There was a robe, a pair of blue pajamas, and a stuffed dog. They seemed depressed and quiet and left early, assuring me that everything was going to be all right. Their faces showed the strain of the day, the strain of pretending. They were not really good with illness, not good at pretending.

Afterward I lay in bed staring out the window. Christmas-tree lights splattered on the pavement, red, black, red, black, as they blinked on and off like a neon sign. Finally I went to sleep, the feel of Jonathan's gold ring on my finger.

On New Year's Eve most people in town have parties. From seven o'clock on at Quiet Oaks you could hear the sound of cars on the highway and see the reflection of moving headlights. Isolated firecrackers went off prematurely; a church bell rang.

Among the nursing staff itself there was an air of weariness, the feeling of a year held too long. It was as if they couldn't wait to tear down all the Chirstmas decorations, be done with the parties, be done with the carols and poinsettias, the visitors, the boxes of chocolates passed around in the nurses' station.

The girls brought us trays of tired turkey and dressing and cranberries as if they were tired of that, too. They went through the business of bathing and brushing of teeth and saying good-nights as if the season had exhausted them completely, as if they would never get through the night. Done with our room now, one of them turned, her hand poised on the light switch. "Happy New Year," she said to me gaily, summoning up some last bit of energy. Even that sounded false from repetition, as if she no longer really believed the words, as if she had shouted Merry Christmas and Happy New Year too many times. She was a tall girl named Barbara with long, stringy hair.

I lay awake as the new year came in. The building was dark and quiet; most of the patients had long ago gone to bed. The few that were left waiting for the new year sat in the dining room playing cards or talking.

At eleven o'clock there was the change of shifts. The time clock clicked as the girls went home. Then there was a burst of laughter, with voices calling out goodnight in the parking lot, the sound of cars starting.

At twelve o'clock a cannon went off in town, and horns began to honk. A church bell in the distance tolled solemnly twelve times. Someplace in town—it might have been at Wilson—there was the *puff-puff* sound of roman candles being shot off. A spray of skyrockets filled the sky, and then one lone blue one like a star falling. After that it was silent again.

And so the year ended, quietly, almost peaceably, and with no hint of what the new year was to bring.

Twelve

At Quiet Oaks the new year started out on a note of briskness. In a surge of energy, the nursing staff removed Christmas decorations, dumped wilted flowers into the garbage, and changed room assignments.

"We're going to move you down to the other end of the hall today," the lead aide said briskly, coming into the room one morning. "You'll be closer to the nurses' station and we can do more for you there."

Astonishingly, two other girls appeared and began now to unhook my portable TV, clear the stand, and pile clothes on top of my bed. They proceeded to clear the room, talking to me as they worked.

A funny feeling began to grow in me as they continued to strip my mobile from the ceiling and pile more clothes on the bed. All the things I had planned to say to Jonathan that afternoon when he came, died in my throat. My mouth felt dry and I swallowed a couple times. They were moving me down to the other end of the building. Why were they moving me down there? That was where they put people who were going to die, wasn't it? Wasn't that what the old lady had said? Did that mean they thought I was going to die?

I wanted Jonathan suddenly; Jonathan would stop them; Jonathan didn't believe in death; Jonathan believed in Atlantis and life and some idealistic code that made men better.

All the time the activity continued around me; the bed beneath me was now rolling cumbrously out of the room, through the doorway, down the hallway. Patients in wheelchairs moved aside. A nurse, coming out of the nurses' lounge, sidestepped and smiled. "How's my favorite patient today?" she said, leaning down.

The bed was heavy with me in it, and the girls paused a moment to rest. "Easy. Get the back end turned around a little more. . . . " They were struggling, aiming the bed toward a doorway.

The doorways of the nursing home had been planned wrong when the building was originally built. A bed could barely be wedged through one. It had to go in absolutely straight and then the sides scraped. I could hear a rubbing sound as rubber gave against the wood; then we had cleared the doorway. A stand was in the way; one of the girls removed it. Then the bed eased its way toward a cleared space by the window.

"I think you'll like it here, Ann," the lead aide said, and smiled at me.

I stiffened. No, I wouldn't like it here. I never in a million

135

years would like it here. They weren't fooling me any with their smiles and softness and whiteness. My glance skittered off the two other beds in the room. Hopeless. Hopeless cases.

The TV had been hooked up again, my bell arranged, clothes put in the closets. They were preparing to leave.

Cold anger swept through me. I jabbed my finger at my Peanuts mobile still lying on the bed, and they hung it up.

"See, Ann. You can see everything from the window," one of the girls said. Her voice was soft and kind. She patted my shoulder. "Rest now and we'll be back."

Rest now. Well, if they thought I was going to rest in this place they were crazy. I sat up in bed, alert now, very alert. I don't know what I expected would happen.

After a half hour I relaxed a little. I wasn't going to die today, this minute. A dry chuckle rose from my throat. Still, I was wary, watching very carefully any movement that went on in the room. At noon the girls came in to feed us—me and the two other patients. It was all very normal and familiar, the same old stuff, Jell-O and a pureed gray mixture, soft foods that bed patients could eat.

A nurse came in with some ice cream, and I let her trickle it down my throat. It tasted surprisingly good. I could have eaten another Dixie cup, but she was getting up to leave. I watched her rise tiredly and pick up the empty cup from the stand. My mouth twisted bleakly. She was no longer interested in me. Already she had relegated me to the world of the dead. The thought dried up the faint feeling of pleasure I'd had in the ice cream and I was suddenly no longer hungry.

I stared out the window waiting for Jonathan. Maybe he wouldn't know what room I was in. Maybe he'd look for me and then go away. I felt my ears straining for the sound of taps on the floor. Then they came. *Clip, clip.*

"Hi, friend," he said as he entered the room.

I lifted my hand.

"Got a window view now, huh? Boy, what a privileged character."

I stared at him suspiciously and didn't answer.

"This is great. Really nice." He peered out the window. "You can see the mountain from here. Look."

I raised my head and looked indifferently. What was so great about seeing the mountain if you were never going there again to ski? If you were never going there again to camp where you would wake up in the morning with the day unbelievably white and the sun in your eyes and the air so cold it stung your throat? What was the good of looking at the mountain when you couldn't be there? I let my head fall back on the bed, disinterested.

Jonathan gave me a quiet, measuring look, as if he had suddenly comprehended my mood.

"You'll be all right," he said in a matter-of-fact voice.

I won't be all right, I thought. I'm going to die. I propped the alphabet board in position and spelled out the words.

"I'm going to die."

Jonathan's face registered shock, then almost immediately impatience. "If you're going to talk that way I'm not going to listen," he said angrily. He swung around, his mouth tightening. "I'm just not going to listen, Ann. You're not going to die. Get that out of your head."

"Might as well face the truth," I muttered inwardly, and I wrote the words on the board. And it was the truth. I was going to die. Everybody knew it but me. Might just as well

137

face it. There would be another blood clot, and another, and one of them would end it, I thought, depressed.

"You're alive," Jonathan said fiercely. "You can think. You can communicate. You're a human being. As long as a person is alive, there's hope. He's still a human being." He spoke shakily, a little embarrassed to be putting such thoughts into words.

A flare of wild impossible hope burst in my chest. Yes, what did they know? They expected everyone to die. They planned on it. It was part of the setup, part of the routine.

"There is no nursing home in Atlantis?" I wrote, trying to make it a joke.

"Right. There is no nursing home in Atlantis. So you can't be in a nursing home, can you? That is a fallacy they try to make you believe," Jonathan said. "They have to maintain the fiction so that they can keep their jobs. But in reality, it isn't a nursing home at all."

"No nurses."

"Right."

"No doctors."

"Right."

"Nobody dies."

"Only those who want to die," Jonathan said. He frowned thoughtfully. "Those who are over a hundred. Those who have done everything they want to do in life and want to die."

I did not believe him for a minute. It was just a part of the giant fabrication he had spun all year at Wilson: a dream, like Atlantis, of how he would have liked the world to be. I looked at his face, set in a frowning-thinking expression. I could feel him making up the story as he went along, improvising, fitting pieces together so they had a certain convincing logic. I almost believed it for a moment.

Then I noticed his hands. They were clenched very tightly on the bedrail. The knuckles were white from the effort of gripping it. The way he wanted it to be—because he couldn't face death. He couldn't face . . . the thought came slowly . . . couldn't face the truth . . . that he had caused it.

My mind swung back to the river. I saw his body arched in the moonlight, saw myself diving. I felt his arms thrashing, pulling me down, and I felt again the surge of anger in my chest. "What are you trying to do, kill us both?" I had shouted that night. But it was I who was going to die. Not him. He would go on and go to the U. He would go on and do all those marvelous things we had planned together. I wouldn't do any of them.

I would never climb the mountain again. I would never go to New York, where the lights splashed like diamonds in the sky and everyone wrote books or plays or Broadway musicals. I would never travel around Europe on a bicycle and eat cheese and bread and wear lederhosen and say *Guten Morgen* solemnly to all the natives. I would never go to any of those places I had read about in books where men wore tuxedos and women wore long gowns and where giant chandeliers hung from the ceilings and you danced all night. Because of him, I would never go to any of those places or do any of those things.

In the next bed one of the roommates roused from her sleep and sat up in bed, hacking horribly, then spitting out a clot of phlegm. Resistance built in my chest. She was going to die. I was going to die, too, I thought with panic. I hated dying. I hated Jonathan for living.

139

"What are you thinking?" Jonathan asked in a curious voice. He smiled, trying to make it a joke. "You act like you just caught me cheating in Casey's test. Your mind is going to explode with all that activity," he said, grinning. "It's going to fly into a million pieces."

If you knew what I was thinking, you would never believe it, I thought. I am thinking such terrible thoughts that you would never believe them.

"Quit staring," Jonathan said. "You look like an owl. I feel like my pants are unzipped or something." He looked down at his slacks. "No, that isn't it. It must be something else."

I grinned wobbly and lifted my hand, acknowledging his humor. My mind raced on. Atlantis was a fake. A giant fake. And Jonathan was a fake, too. The biggest fake of all. I felt cheated, as if I had been duped by a carnival barker, handed a piece of pink cotton candy only to discover it had melted into sugar and nothingness.

"Okay, out with it," Jonathan said crisply. He turned his back and faced the window.

I stared at his slender back. Did he think I would ever tell him my thoughts? Did he think I would say them out loud? And then I realized something else. It was not his fault. It was simply not in his character to accept the truth. He could no more believe in death than he could believe in the moon falling from the sky. Atlantis had been real to him. It was still real to him.

It was I who had changed—I who no longer believed in that island where people lived by the ideal of perfection. Like the real Atlantis, Jonathan's Atlantis had sunk into the sea.

Jonathan took a new tack. "I saw Akins and Coster today."

I lifted my eyebrows.

140

"Home for the holidays. Both very big on campus, I take it."

I smiled feebly, glad for the reprieve from my violent thoughts.

"Very collegiate. Very much the worldly college men. Coster smokes a pipe now."

I smiled at the thought of Coster smoking a pipe. *Thump-thump.*   "What's he going to be?"

"Oh, a psychiatrist," Jonathan said, lifting his voice importantly, expanding his chest. "What else?"

I laughed out loud. I could see Coster in the role, slightly superior, puffing thoughtfully on a pipe as he diagnosed a patient.

"Akins is going for veterinarian. He's all set up with his uncle when he gets out."

Did Jonathan wish he were there, too, walking across a green lawn smoking a pipe, affecting a collegiate manner? I looked at him sharply. Was there regret in his face?

That was it! I thought, shocked. He wanted to go on. Without me. I stared at him, my mind a turmoil. It was hopeless, and he wanted to go on without me.

A moment ago, I had been angry at him for not believing in death; now I was angry at him because I thought he did believe in it. He was tired of playing games with me. He wanted to go on without me. It was the truth. It had to be the truth. Jonathan was not so stupid that he didn't know what moving to this end of the hall meant. Special care. What a crock of baloney. He knew as everyone else knew. He was smiling and pretending just exactly as the nurses had. See the pretty window. See Spot. See the dog run, I thought, the thoughts tumbling out of my mind chaotically now. See Dick. See Jane. See the mountain.

Stop lying! Stop this insane lying! I thought. You don't want me to live any more than the rest of them do. You want me to die, so you can go on and live your life. So you can go on and be a big man at the U!

I was trembling, I was so angry. I reached for the water pitcher and swung my arm, and it crashed against the wall, water slopping down the side.

"Ge-o!" I sobbed. "Ge-o!" But no real words came from my throat, only the gibberish.

Jonathan stared at the water pitcher and at the water, which was making little rivers down the side of the wall. He stiffened. Then casually he walked over and picked the pitcher up and replaced it on the stand.

"Talk to me, Ann. Tell me what you're thinking!" he said urgently. "Tell me what you want. Spell it out on the board."

He was urging the alphabet board into my hand as if I were a first grader, pointing his finger at the letters as if I were an idiot who couldn't understand how to use it. All the time he was talking to me in a quiet, reasonable voice, which, I realized in that long, terrible second, was exactly the same tone of voice everyone else in the place used—a tone of voice Jonathan had never used before.

A combination of frustration and hate welled in my throat as I looked at his lean, intelligent, healthy face. I hated dying. I hated being cajoled. I hated him.

My fingers jabbed at the board, sure and definite. My chest froze to stone.

G-E-T O-U-T!

Jonathan stared at the board. There was a long, tension-filled silence. Then, without looking at me, he turned and stiffly walked out of the room.

Thirteen

G*et out!* I had screamed. And he had gone; disappeared as if he'd gone up in smoke.

I took a curious, morbid interest in the death of an old lady in my room. She was old and meant nothing to me, yet how she died held interest for me now. In fact, it was the only interest I had. Dying was the most important and interesting event in life, I thought hysterically. The only event. I don't know how this had escaped me before. The act of dying was the only important thing there was in life. It was the one single thing that joined all men. All of life led to this one day, this one moment—death. Yet people completely ignored it. They lived their whole life as if it were never to be. They should have been given courses in universities on the subject, I thought. They should have forced youngsters to look at the faces of the dead as part of their education, a prerequisite for graduation. I felt as exhilarated as if I had made some important discovery.

I lay awake listening to the bubble of the oxygen tank. The sound filled the room. The woman already was more dead than alive, like a dry stick drawing in a breath, letting it out—drawing in a breath, letting it out. Finally, in the middle of the night, some time between two and three, the sound stopped.

The next day I had a relapse and felt fear and terrible depression. There came back to me the smell of spring, Jonathan's face, the feel of sun and water, the sight of Martha's Peak. A hundred scenes rose in my mind: Jonathan and I walking along a sidewalk, the touch of the sun on the mountains, the sound of frogs croaking, the feel of Jonathan's hand clamped over mine.

In the darkness that night my teeth began to chatter with fear. I looked over at the empty bed where the woman had died and was afraid to go to sleep for fear I wouldn't wake up. I hid the sleeping pill the nurse gave me under my tongue and pretended to swallow it. In the morning I was still staring open-eyed at the window when dawn came.

"You have a visitor," one of the nurses said. *Jonathan?*

But it was not Jonathan. It was Carol Marshall. I gestured and showed her I had to use the board to communicate. A funny expression crossed her face, and hope died in my chest. It was not love she felt, but pity.

"Oh, Ann—" she said. Her lip trembled and she started to cry.

Her pity dried up the hope, dried up the chattering fear. I didn't need her pity. When you came right down to it, maybe I was the lucky one. Love, desire, hope, promises—

all those earthly chains that bound her no longer held me. I was completely free. Not she.

I felt myself grow calm, and the remembrance of the old lady's death no longer disturbed me. I was so calm, in fact, that I found myself saying to Mother the next day, "When I die—"

"Oh, Ann, how can you talk about—" The thought upset her, and she pulled out a handkerchief and started to cry.

Her tears startled me. I apologized quickly, but all evening she was upset, and she left early.

On bath day at six o'clock in the morning, the girls came in to awaken my other roommate. "Come on, Mrs. Reeves. It's time for your shower," they said. "Mrs. Reeves."

The old lady didn't stir. They pulled her out of bed and started taking off the gown and wrapping her in a bath blanket. I watched them put her in the shower chair. She looked like a mummy wrapped in the blanket, ready for the shower; her eyes were still closed. She looked groggy from sleep as they wheeled her out.

A few minutes later they came back with the dripping figure and whisperingly concluded that she didn't look very well, that she looked sort of green, sort of dead. A nurse came in and confirmed the fact that she was dead.

All the time, of course, she had been dead. She must have died in the night. In their haste, in their inexperience, they thought she was only still sleeping and had taken her down to the shower.

I could not help myself. I burst out laughing. Several times during the day a chuckle would rise in my throat and I would start laughing again, unable to control the sound.

The following day a man was wheeled out of a room,

145

presumably dead. He was pronounced dead, and then, two minutes later, he groaned, and sat up. I burst into laughter again, laughing until tears rolled down my cheeks. I couldn't stop.

My parents visited me that afternoon and I broke down completely. "Get me out of here," I begged, clinging to their hands.

My parents were disturbed, but in the end they were helpless. Unused to a life of any kind except one for pleasure, they did not know how to cope with death. They were embarrassed and pained, and helpless.

I calmed down enough to assure them I was all right. When they left I felt terribly depressed. I was alone. Everyone in the nursing home was sympathetic, and that was depressing, too. I turned my back and stared out the window at the mountain.

The hope of reprieve, of a miracle, of escaping dominated my thoughts all afternoon. I refused to join in any activitity. I plotted to get a message to Dr. Anderson. Somehow I must force him to take me back into that world of living.

Later in the day a minister came to visit and I refused to listen as he talked about joining God in heaven. I wanted to lie in the sunshine. I wanted Jonathan.

"You do believe in God, don't you?" he said.

I thumped out Y-E-S on the board, an I-suppose-so kind of yes. I realized that was what he expected me to say.

Looking startled, he pointed at the alphabet board. "That's quite ingenious," he said. His Adam's apple was very prominent and had a curious way of bobbing up and down in his neck as he talked. "Really. Quite ingenious." He remembered that he had been talking about God. "You believe in God. And heaven," he prompted.

I started to say that heaven was out. I just couldn't believe in heaven or angels, but the difficulty of communicating was too great.

He turned it into a sermon, not waiting for my answer. "So you know there is nothing to fear. God will take care of you."

I suppose he was sincere, yet something about the tone of his voice sounded so phony that I was suddenly angry and belligerent. I looked at him coldly. Actually, I said, I found death quite interesting.

He looked startled again. "Interesting?" he said.

"Yes."

"Yes, well—" He cleared his throat. "You're young. You probably don't realize the seriousness of death," he said gently.

I said I was perfectly aware what death meant. It meant that there was nothing.

"My dear child," he said.

"Nothing." I stamped the letters out emphatically on the board. I thought of Jonathan, sunlight, water. Nothing, I thought. Nothing.

"For a young person you're very bitter," he said. He seemed to forget that he was a minister and that he was there to console me, and he became almost angry then. His face got red as he said that he had never seen anyone so bitter—and so selfish.

I wanted to say that I hadn't asked him here, that I was trying to adjust to things the best I could. It was I, not he, who was dying. If I wanted to be bitter, it was my choice. How I died was my choice. Mine. Not the nursing home's choice. Not my parents' choice. Mine. My chest was heaving. I wanted to shout at him to get out, just get out and leave me alone. I wanted to be alone. I liked being alone.

"I'll come back again," he said gently. He patted my hand. His own hand was strangely soft and warm. "Don't forget. God is always with you." He looked into my eyes earnestly.

Then he was gone, hurrying out of the room. I heard him speak to one of the nurses. One of the patients called out sweetly, "Operator. Op-er-a-tor—" And then darkness came over the mountain and the day ended.

I looked at the empty bed on the other side of the room. My lip quivered; I could feel my teeth begin to chatter slightly. I clamped my mouth shut firmly and began to count the squares in the wallpaper.

Fourteen

S sanity came back with the entrance of Jonathan into the room Friday afternoon. He was wearing a starched white shirt and dark slacks, his hair was brushed neatly, his shoes tapped energetically on the floor, and he was smiling his intelligent, civilized smile.

"I'm sorry I haven't been in," he said. "Mother had an errand in Portland. We were down there until yesterday."

My outburst hadn't driven him away. He had been in Portland. That is why he hadn't come to see me. Portland. My chest expanded with the clean feel of relief.

"Did you have a good time?" I spelled, suddenly feeling light-hearted and conversational.

"Fair." He shrugged. "I went to the library one day, and I went to Jantzen Beach and Portland Meadows. I lost two dollars on a horse race." He grinned. "The horse's name was

Oats. You might know with a name like that what kind of a horse it was." He looked at me critically, quizzically. "You?"

"Lovely time, too."

"I bet." He lifted his eyebrows toward the nursing station and rolled his eyes in a gesture of despair. Suddenly his glance fell on a piece of paper above my bed. "What is *that?*"

The sign above my bed said that this patient was in the Reality Orientation program. Every morning I was to be asked my name, what month it was, what day it was. I felt humiliated even to look at it, and I stared down at the bed, ashamed.

"Unbelievable!" Jonathan said. "You haven't lost your *mind!* For crying out loud, you're not *senile!*" He reached up and tore the paper off the wall, crumpled it in his fist, and dropped it into a wastebasket. "So much for Reality Orientation," he said lightly.

They would put another one back tomorrow, but still it pleased me strangely.

He looked back at my face more soberly. "Any response from the old motor center?"

I shook my head. Nothing was coming back. My hand was a little stronger maybe, but that probably came from practice. I could swallow easier. Otherwise, nothing.

Jonathan nodded. He didn't say anything for a long moment; then he stood up and faced the window, standing the way he always stood when he was going to say something serious.

"When people die," he said in a low voice, "I believe that someone rises up to take their place." He spoke with difficulty, not looking at me, but with the familiar, sharp ring of conviction in his voice. "If I were to die, someone would

150

rise up and take my place—finish what I had started. Not now. Maybe generations from now."

He continued to look out the window. "It's like Atlantis," he said. "It sank into the sea, but I rose up one day—and carried on. So those people there did not really die, and Atlantis did not die. I believe that's the way it is in life. A person dies, and someone rises up to take his place."

It was a surprising statement. Perhaps Jonathan had made it all up in that moment just for me. It is possible, but I do not believe that either. I believe that it was something he had believed all the time, but only in that moment said out loud because he knew that I was worried about dying.

It was typical of Jonathan that he did not say something phony or avoid the subject or pretend like everybody else that I wasn't going to die. I loved him for that.

Jonathan turned around and faced me.

"I almost died once," he said. "I had T.B. That's why I missed a year of school. I thought a lot about death in that year."

I was surprised about the T.B. No one had ever mentioned it and I had finally accepted the school gossip that he had missed a year of school because of a nervous breakdown. That hadn't been true at all. He'd had T.B.

"Don't accept my idea," Jonathan said carelessly, making it not important.

I said I hadn't thought about death much (that wasn't quite true. It was the only thing I'd thought about since the last time I'd seen him). I didn't mind dying so much, I said, I just wanted to do it my own way. Then we changed the subject and went on to something else. It was the only time, the one and only time Jonathan and I ever talked about death.

"I went to a basketball game with Akins last night," Jonathan said. "The U has a big seven-foot center. Akins is pretty keen on him."

"How is he?"

"Tall." Jonathan grinned. "About as fast as a man on stilts. He spent most of his time on the floor. I saw Coster, too. He doesn't have anything to do with sports now or games, naturally. Everything is up here now." He tapped his forehead.

I grinned.

"You remember Raymond Summers, don't you?"

"Yes," I nodded after a moment, feeling awkward.

"Well, he ended up at the U. Very big in the art department. He's got a beard and wears his hair long and straight. I guess he'll fit in there. He never quite fit in at Wilson."

I didn't answer. I don't think he expected an answer. I remembered that night at the party, the two boys dancing. It seemed like a long time ago. I was older now, more mature; it no longer meant anything. Raymond Summers no longer meant anything, and never had really, I realized. He had never threatened Jonathan's and my relationship; I had only felt threatened.

There was a little silence. Jonathan awkwardly picked up the stuffed dog on my bed. "How many of these things do you have? It's like a *zoo*, for crying out loud!" he said, and the moment passed. A nurse came in with medicine, and he told me a joke about doctors he'd heard.

It was growing dark outside. The last rays of the sun had hit the mountain, and it turned pinkish like strawberry ice cream. Then the sun's light gradually left it, and it became cool and blue.

"Well, I'd better be going," Jonathan said uncertainly.

I picked up the alphabet board to tell him there was something else I wanted to say. I didn't look at him as I thumped out the letters.

"You better go on to the U without me."

Jonathan looked at me sharply. Then he shrugged. "I think I'll hang around awhile yet," he said casually, looking away.

We both knew that he'd have to go on alone someday, yet I felt absurdly grateful for his words. Strangely, it was Jonathan who spoiled any plan I might have had to accept death. I clung to him as I clung to my stuffed animals on my bed. Sometimes at night my mind would be flooded with the memory of him, scenes so real that they could have been movie clips—Jonathan rising into the air, clearing the high bar; Jonathan's clips going down the halls of Wilson; Jonathan moving through the summer in his easy, slouchy stride.

And spring was coming again. The bushes outside the windows shot out new green. Waking up in the morning I heard birds chirping outside the windows. The chattering racket continued all day as they began to build nests under the eaves. In the field outside my window, children played tag; the days were getting longer.

I could talk in a faltering, clumsy way now. I took that as a sign that I would recover. My heart leaped with a wild, impossible joy one day when I said a word perfectly. I could talk. *Talk*, I thought, hope flooding over me. A cry of happiness rose in my throat.

Then one day I stared at the walls and I knew it wasn't true. There had been a small, infinitesimal change, that was all. Since then there had been nothing. I could make myself understood, that was all. I wouldn't be going to the U in the fall. Jonathan would be going; I would never go.

Yet I clung to Jonathan selfishly, not wanting him to have life if I couldn't have it, too.

"Let him go," my father said gently one day.

I looked at him sullenly and didn't answer.

"He won't go on without you," my father said. "Can't you see that, Ann?"

"He'll go on," I mumbled, "when he's ready."

You could not make Jonathan do anything he didn't want to do. I had learned that long ago. His mind had a strange logic of its own.

But it was true also that he felt guilty. Sometimes I would catch him off guard silently watching me with an indescribable heavy pain in his lean, intelligent face; then I would know he was thinking that he had caused it, that if it hadn't been for him panicking, I would be well now. I thought I detected a longing in his voice now sometimes when he talked jokingly about the University and Coster and Akins. He always talked about the University in a certain way, always making Coster and Akins comic characters with their new collegiate manners. I felt that this was a pose, a veneer of casualness to hide his true feelings that he wished he were free to be with them.

And he remembered, too, that I had never forgiven him. One day the words slipped out as we were joking about something else. "If you do, I'll never forgive you," I cried.

Jonathan's hand grew very still on the bedrail. He looked at me with a strange expression on his face, almost as if I had slapped him. The light from the setting sun shone on his face and made him look vulnerable.

Then one day Jonathan said, "I don't know. Maybe I won't go on to college."

I looked at him quickly. It was impossible to tell what he was thinking. His face was blank and expressionless.

"I think you should," I said. "Definitely."

"Why?"

"You've got a good mind. You might do something great."

"That's true," he said, grinning. "I have a terrific mind. It would be a shame to waste it—but I don't know."

"You're just afraid of the competition," I said. "You had everything your way at good old Wilson, and the U is a big, big puddle. You might be just a little frog in it. It scares you."

He grinned.

"You don't want to play if you can't be best," I gibed. "You'll pack up your football and go home."

That's when he liked me best, when I was teasing him. He continued to smile, his face cheerful and confident, ready for the next gibe.

"You're spoiled," I said.

He continued to look at me with his brown eyes. "I don't think I'll go," he said. "I think I'll wait for you. We'll go together."

"What am I, your personal cheering section?" I said angrily. I swung my arm. "Can't you do anything without me? If you're waiting for me, you're crazy. I wouldn't wait for you."

Jonathan cocked his head to one side. "I bet you would," he said. "You're just dumb enough—and you've got this crush on me. Yeah, you'd probably wait."

"I don't know that I would. As for having a crush, that's just your egotism."

155

"Oh? I thought you liked me. I thought I fascinated you."

I snorted.

He grinned. "Now you know if I went without you, your feelings would be hurt. You'd lie here in your little zoo and not talk to anyone. Nope, you can't do without me."

"Can't do without you! Boy! What egotism! Do you think I need you around to function?" And then I stopped short as I realized the whole point of the conversation had been to get my reaction. Jonathan was testing the wind to see how I really felt. It was almost summer. He was thinking ahead to fall, which was only three months away.

"Seriously," I said, "I think you should go this fall. If you put it off much longer you're going to be gray-haired by the time you graduate." I picked up my stuffed dog and rearranged it on the bed. "If you're worried about me I'll get along—here in my little zoo," I said cheerfully.

"Ann—"

"Yes?" I had the impression he was going to say something important.

"Nothing." He decided against the question, leaned down, and patted the stuffed dog on the head. "Good night, Puddles," he said, and left the room.

I lay in bed watching darkness come into the room. Making my mind blank, I counted the cracks in the wall, the number of pictures in the room, the number of trips a certain nurse made down the hall. The possibilities were unexciting but unlimited.

Later in the night there were other diversions: identifying various patients by their voices, seeing if I could guess the time, counting the number of breaths my roommates took, counting the clicks of the time clock as aides checked in and out, seeing if I could estimate the time the aides would take to finish a round.

The night aides always took a break after the round. I could hear them eating their lunch at two o'clock. Their voices would float across the hall from the nurse's lounge, and sometimes if I strained my ears I could hear what they said. On the whole, that wasn't satisfactory, because I could only catch an occasional word or two.

Gradually I got so I didn't listen to them. The diversion of monotonously counting the cracks in the wall was more satisfactory. I came to know every visible article in the room—vases, flowers, pictures. They became familiar and satisfying. When people died and their belongings were stripped from the walls I felt lost and disoriented for a few days. I even missed the old people themselves—their rackety breathing, their clattering false teeth, their odd mannerisms.

Obviously any place that you live in long enough, no matter how small or restrictive, eventually becomes home.

Fifteen

I had the room alone for three days, then a stroke patient was moved in and, one day in July, a woman named Frances Castleman. She was different from any of the others I had had as roommates, because she was rather young, and so normal and healthy-looking that at first I couldn't understand why she had been put there. Her skin was clear and lightly powdered, and she had a bright, cheerful tone of voice.

Almost immediately she began talking.

"Hello. I'm Frances Castleman," she said, smiling in a friendly way.

"Ann—Ann Taylor," I mumbled.

"I hope we'll be friends." She smiled again and gazed critically around the room. "It's small but it's cheerful. And there's lots of light."

I didn't answer. She began to arrange her belonging on the

158

stand and bed around her. A large box of tissues she placed by her hand. She also had a box of pictures, which she took out and began to look through.

"Last year at this time I was in Europe," she said. "As healthy as anyone. It's hard to believe that in such a short time—" She stopped herself. "Oh, here's one of me at the Eiffel Tower. Don't I look like the tourist, though?" She laughed and handed me the picture across the rails.

I looked at a woman with dark glasses and a camera slung over her shoulder posing in front of the famous landmark. The picture was a Polaroid with over-bright green grass and blue sky, and it looked like every other picture of a tourist I had ever seen.

"I have this rather rare disease." She said the name of it. "It progresses very fast."

I looked at her, trying to think of something to say.

"Oh, don't feel sorry for me," she said quickly. "I've had so many things in life—and I'm so glad now I took that trip. I went with two friends. We had such a splendid time." She sighed. "Paris in the springtime. It's everything they say it is. I'd love to be there now. Instead of here." She made a face and looked around the room.

"I know what you mean," I said. I handed the picture back.

"You can look at the rest of the pictures sometime if you like," she offered. She added with droll humor, "I am displayed prominently in all of them."

I laughed.

"I'm so glad you're young," she said. "I like your little menagerie."

"My zoo, Jonathan calls it."

"Your boyfriend?"

"Just a friend."

"I see." She continued to look at the pictures. "What's our roommate's name?"

I had to think a minute. "Audrey Johnson," I said. She was sleeping, but my voice fell to a whisper. "Stroke patient. She talks all the time about going home."

"Ah, that's bad. A stroke."

"She won't go home."

The young woman's eyebrows lifted. "Well, you never know," she said calmly. "Sometimes these things come back rather surprisingly." She looked at the sleeping woman's face, then back at me. "How old are you?"

"Nineteen."

"I'm fifty-five. From your perspective I suppose that seems old. I really don't feel old. I used to think that forty was ancient." She laughed again merrily.

"No, you don't seem old," I said slowly.

It was nice having company in the room, and we became good friends in the next weeks. I looked at all of her pictures and she told me about her life. She had been an army nurse when she was young. During World War II, she had been in the Pacific. She had talked to MacArthur and been to Japan, and she told me many stories of the war.

When she ate she had great difficulty in swallowing and she sucked on ice chips all day instead of drinking water. Sometimes she would choke, and then her dark eyes would be still and frightened. That was how she would eventually die, by choking, she told me one day.

"I hope I die gracefully," she said. "That I don't make a big fuss."

"I'd rather make a fuss," I said with relish. "A good knock-down fight."

She laughed.

"They hate it so here when anyone puts up a fuss. It throws them into a real tailspin when someone doesn't follow their rules."

"Well, you can see their point of view," she said, laughing again, amused. The exertion made her start to choke. Her face got red, then blue, and she gasped for breath. Then gradually she recovered and was all right.

"I have to be careful," she said apologetically.

"I'm sorry," I said awkwardly.

"Oh, don't stop laughing. I love to hear it."

Neither of us laughed three days later. Incredibly our roommate Audrey Johnson, the stroke patient, began to pack her belongings; she was going home. Her relatives came; she dressed in her best clothes, got into her wheelchair, and prepared to leave.

"Good-bye, Ann. Good-bye, Frances. You'll be going home soon, too." In a burst of belated goodwill, the crabby old lady wheeled about the room, shaking our hands and smiling.

"Good-bye. Good luck." I had trouble remembering her name, then did.

Everything was very quiet in the room after she left. Frances looked straight ahead and said nothing. I couldn't think of anything to say either. Because of some accident of fate we wouldn't be going home. A stroke patient, who had seemed always much nearer death than we, had got up and started to walk and was on her way home.

Frances finally said she was tired, closed her eyes and went

161

to sleep. I lay in bed staring out the window. I couldn't sleep, disturbed by the fact that someone so disabled had recovered and gone home. A month later, when Frances died, I sobbed wildly and uncontrollably.

What was the good of knowing them? I thought bitterly. They just died. August came and I stared out the window at the mountain. The snow had melted from it so that it no longer looked like an ice-cream cone. Shadows at the base were blue and gray, with the brown of summer.

The nurses found me cold and strange now and ceased to joke with me or try to coax me into laughter. I stared at them without speaking, and they left the room quickly, suddenly afraid of me. Sometimes I stared at them just for perversity to make them uncomfortable. Once I had been their pet. Now that affection was gone, and there was awkward silence between us as I grew sullen and uncooperative.

The sight of the aides coming up the walk in the morning brought only a vague curiosity as to whether they'd wave or not. It made no difference. I would not wave back. I rejected them all. It was the one privilege I had, to die any way I chose—sullen, laughing, or bitter. Any way I chose, I thought. And I chose to be difficult. I chose. It was my choice. I would not play their game. I had been happy. I had loved sunshine and water. Now I was unhappy to die.

"All right, don't talk. Who cares!" an aide snapped at me one day. "If you don't want friends, it's okay with me." She turned back from the door, stricken. "I'm sorry Ann. I—"

I stared at her, childishly unforgiving.

One day late in August Jonathan came to see me. I was sullen and said something cutting to him. In the midst of a sentence his voice broke and he started to cry, putting his hands over his face, his shoulders shaking silently.

"Why is the world such a rotten place?" he sobbed. He stared at me belligerently, his face ugly with emotion. His features were distorted, twisted out of shape, and there were tears running down his cheeks. He looked like the broken image that you see when you look down into the river. "Such a damn lousy place!" he choked.

It was the moment, I think, when Jonathan really faced the fact for the first time that I wasn't going to get well. For all of his courage, he could not overcome this one thing. I thought back to that day when he had said with such clear certainty, "I would have broken."

That night my mind flew in all directions. Always in one part of me I had counted on Jonathan to perform some miracle. It had never occurred to me that there were things that even he could not do.

Since Frances' death, I had abandoned my friendships. Any roommates that I had now never spoke to me. Maybe they thought I couldn't speak. Maybe they thought I was some sort of deaf-mute.

I looked out the window at the mountain. It was Sunday afternoon, one of those terrible Sunday afternoons at Quiet Oaks. The mountain seemed remote and inhuman, one of those gigantic monuments that have no real relationship to life, existing only to belong in tourists' photograph albums.

In desperation I turned and tried to talk to the old woman in the next bed.

"Shall we go out in the hall for a while?" I said.

She ignored me.

"I think they're playing bingo. Would you like to play

bingo?" I said desperately in a louder voice, remembering that she was hard of hearing.

The old lady looked vaguely at some spot behind my shoulder, then turned back to the bed again and began to knit on her afghan. "Would someone turn the TV off? I don't like that program," she said.

The hair on my scalp lifted slowly. TV. She thought I was on the TV set. I had ignored her for so long that she didn't recognize me as a human being. I was part of the furniture.

Until Frances had died there had always been the hope of a reprieve. I did not realize how much I had counted on it. But with the end of summer the door to hope seemed to close. Melodramatically I thought perhaps I might kill myself—save up my pills or slash my wrists with a razor blade. The possibilities floated through my mind, and I discarded them one by one as either too bloody or too impractical.

My parents came in for a few minutes, on their way to dinner with friends.

"Would you rather we stayed here all day, Ann?" Mother said, looking at my face closely.

"No. Go ahead."

"We don't have to go."

"I'll be all right."

Jonathan wasn't coming in tonight. He had joined a team and was playing baseball; tonight was a semi-playoff game. I thought perversely that it was a good excuse not to have to come to see me. I hated him for living. I hated dying.

A nurse came in with a needle. "What's that? Poison?" I said sarcastically.

Wearily, patience tried to the limit, she answered in a tone

I wasn't supposed to hear. "It's strychnine. We give it to all our favorite patients."

I heard that, I thought triumphantly. I heard that. "Someday you'll die, too," I said bitterly.

She was a big woman with a soft, kind face who, to be truthful, had never hurt me. "Practically everyone here is worse off than you, Ann. They still manage to behave like decent human beings," she said gently.

"I have my pride," I said sullenly. And I had loved life more than they, I thought fiercely.

"Everybody here wants to be your friend. You shut them out."

"I don't need anyone," I muttered.

"Fine. Just continue to act like you've been acting. But don't expect anyone to love you," she said crisply. "Stay alone. Hate us—but don't expect people to love you for it. They're only human."

I stared at her, my heart pounding. They're tired of your sullen silences, I thought. They're tired of your selfishness. They no longer care if you live or die. The thought shocked me. Most of my life had been spent being popular, making people like me. What was life for if not to please? I stared at the clouds massed in the sky outside. There was a wind, and the clouds were moving very fast, veritably racing across the sky like a charging, angry gray mob intent on murder. My heart was racing also. Jonathan is tired of you, too, I thought.

In that lonely season, in that loneliest of places; in that season when hate and love were so hopelessly intertwined that I didn't know whether I hated or loved, Jonathan came every day. Because he was Jonathan, he would never admit, even to himself, any restlessness or desire to be free.

Outwardly, if anything, he had become even more faithful, more cheerful. Coster and Akins and all the others were home for the summer. Jonathan mimicked them, made their antics seem hilarious and comic, and it was those overly bright attempts at humor and casualness that made me realize finally that I held him in bondage—a bondage from which only I could release him.

Big decisions, contrary to common belief, are usually made easily, spontaneously. There is almost a spurious quality about them, since of course one has been thinking about them for a long period of time, anyway. The decision has long ago been debated and decided in some deep courtroom of the mind; it only requires the proper moment to rise to the surface.

The day was one of those blustery days that come sometimes in the fall shortly before school starts. Wind alternated with rain and a flying of leaves from the trees, and the sky had the look that is peculiar to fall—a gray, sullen scowl that is not quite menacing yet, but seems to say, Wait a few months! Just wait! Then watch out!

Jonathan came in, in a dark mood. He let the baseball mitt fall onto a chair.

"We lost the game," he said. "One run."

All the brightness of Atlantis had disappeared from his face. He looked tired, already defeated by a winter that hadn't yet arrived with its dark skies and eternal dripping rains, its brooding fogs. His drooping shoulders said that any victory was impossible.

"Have you registered yet?" I asked.

"I'm not going," Jonathan said sullenly. "I thought you understood that."

"What do you mean, you're not going?"

"Let's not talk about it—let's just skip it, okay?"

"If you don't go," I said quietly, looking down at the covers on the bed, "I'll never forgive you for what you did."

Jonathan looked startled. I realized that it was the first time we'd ever mentioned the word, *forgiveness*.

A strange look came over his face. "You never did forgive me, did you, Ann? You said you did, but you never did." He was looking out the window, his back to me.

"I hated the thought of being here," I said. I looked at his back. He wore a black-and-white shirt that looked like a checkerboard. It was hard to speak the words that I had held in me so long. "It's all right now. I want you to go. And I forgive you. For everything. I want you to know that."

"I'm not going anyplace without you, Ann. Will you get that out of your head?" Jonathan said savagely.

"I'd like a party before you go," I said, ignoring him. "A party for everyone." I looked down at the bed and picked at a piece of lint. "I've been rather difficult this month, and I'd like to make it up."

He looked at me doubtfully. I thought he was going to refuse. Instead he nodded. "I guess we could have a party."

"We could have games, music. Maybe someone from Wilson could play the piano, put on a skit or something—"

"Leave that part to me," Jonathan said. He frowned, warming up to the idea a little. It was the place where he was the best: organizing, marshaling the troops.

When he left I stared out the window. Now that the words had been said I felt better. The cliché is quite true; forgiving is good for the soul.

It was the only party that I ever gave unselfishly for others, the only party in my whole life when I didn't wear a new dress. I went to it in a wheelchair, with a stiff collar around my neck.

Afterward Jonathan and I were alone in the room. He continued to talk about the party, steering away from anything serious.

"I think they really enjoyed it. I think they really got a kick out of it."

"It's about time you thought about school," I said sternly. "It starts next week, doesn't it?"

Jonathan didn't answer. Turning, he faced the window, his shoulders set in characteristic stubbornness. I had the feeling that anything I said would be met with stony resistance.

Only a lie would change his mood, so I lied, or half lied. Anything Jonathan believed I could never quite disbelieve, so perhaps it was not entirely a lie.

"You remember once you said, someone rises up and takes your place—well, I believe that's true," I said in a low voice. "If I were to die someone would rise up and take my place. So I don't mind—and I really want you to go."

He waited so long to speak that I thought he had forgotten what I said. His whole attention seemed focused on the mountain as if there in its snowy peak he had suddenly discovered something fascinating. His voice was strange, like someone speaking under water.

"If I go, you won't give up?"

"No."

"All right, I'll go," Jonathan said in a low voice, deciding. "But only because you want me to."

I nodded.

"I'll come back and see you every weekend."

"I'd rather you wouldn't. I'd rather say good-bye now."

"Now look—" Jonathan protested, swinging around.

"There are some things in life a person has to do alone," I said.

"I'll be here," he insisted. "I won't leave you."

"No. I want to do this alone."

Jonathan, who always understood when I was serious, understood now that I really meant it. He nodded. He turned his back on me and continued to stare out the window. His shoulders shook, and I knew he was fighting emotion.

"I love you," he said in a choked voice.

I nodded, my throat suddenly tight. *I know.*

After a second he turned, stooped over, and kissed me.

"Good-bye, Ann," he said.

"Good-bye, Jonathan," I whispered.

"Good-bye, Puddles." He leaned down and patted the stuffed dog on my bed. And then, tears running down his face, he left the room quickly, not turning back. I heard the *clip clip* of his heels going down the hall.

Sixteen

I never saw him again. It was typical of Jonathan's integrity that he would never desert anyone; neither would he violate my decision now. I do not know if he went on to college and entranced some other class of students or not. Perhaps Atlantis was an idea that could come only once in one's life, in a particular time. Perhaps the rest of Jonathan's life would be ordinary—but I always saw him as unique, someone who created a special world of Atlantis, where all of us lived for one year.

Because of Jonathan, I could never quite see the ordinary world in the same way as before. I joined the others in the dining room, where we shuffled cards and laughed and talked, but I never deluded myself that it had anything to do with the real world. Anything at all.

Then one night, a week after I said good-bye to Jonathan, I didn't go down to the dining room with the others. It was the end of September, the day college was to start—a symbolic time, it seemed to me.

I took off the friendship ring and put it in a box in my drawer. Taking all the stuffed animals off my bed, I had a nurse pack them in boxes and store them above my clothes in my closet. I took down the mobile and pennants from the walls, stripping everything away.

It had no real significance, of course, but perhaps symbolically it meant that I had stripped myself bare, too, had shed all of those things that had held me prisoner in life.

Stripped and bare, with only the clean spartan sheet and coarse gray institution blanket over me, I felt strangely clean and satisfied and at peace. I could have taken a different way, but I had been spoiled. I had known Jonathan; I had seen Atlantis.

There in the summer night I held to memory for one last time and then I whispered, "Good-bye, Atlantis," and I relinquished it forever.

The red streaks in the sky faded in the west, and there was the sound, familiar and comforting, of wheelchairs softly going down the hall through the quiet dusk, and the sweet, strange voices of souls floating out from the mainland to sea. I had been happy. I was still happy, this minute, looking out a window, waiting.

The stars came out. Behind them the sky was dark. Black. I hoped for nothing. Wanted nothing. Expected nothing. My life was over. They would find when they washed me only a naked body. The sunshine and water and laughter I loved—I gave away: Jonathan, the high mark, the memory of

171

green-filled days—freely, of my own choice, I gave them all away. To the living.

I kept only one thing: the image of a shining, splendid island that thousands of years ago sank into the sea.